Ben Jonson's The Fountain of Self-Love, or Cynthia's Revels: A Retelling

David Bruce

Published by David Bruce, 2022.

BEN JONSON'S THE FOUNTAIN OF SELF-LOVE, OR CYNTHIA'S REVELS: A RETELLING

First edition. July 10, 2022.

Copyright © 2022 David Bruce.

ISBN: 979-8201509743

Written by David Bruce.

Table of Contents

Cover Photograph for Ben Jonson's *The Fountain of Self-Love, or Cynthia's Revels:* A Retelling

(Quarto Version, year 1600)

Photographer: Jerzy Gorecki

https://pixabay.com/photos/girl-mirror-portrait-character-4310391/

Dedicated to Carl Eugene Bruce and Josephine Saturday Bruce

***

Educate Yourself

Read Like A Wolf Eats

Be Excellent to Each Other

Books Then, Books Now, Books Forever

***

In this retelling, as in all my retellings, I have tried to make the work of literature accessible to modern readers who may lack some of the knowledge about mythology, religion, and history that the literary work's contemporary audience had.

Do you know a language other than English? If you do, I give you permission to translate this book, copyright your translation, publish or self-publish it, and keep all the royalties for yourself. (Do give me credit, of course, for the original retelling.)

I would like to see my retellings of classic literature used in schools, so I give permission to the country of Finland (and all other countries) to buy one copy of this eBook and give copies to all students forever. I also give permission to the state of Texas (and all other states) to buy one copy of this eBook and give copies to all students forever. I also give permission to all teachers to buy one copy of this eBook and give copies to all students forever.

Teachers need not actually teach my retellings. Teachers are welcome to give students copies of my eBooks as background material. For example, if they are teaching Homer's *Iliad* and *Odyssey*, teachers are welcome to give students copies of my *Virgil's* Aeneid: *A Retelling in Prose* and tell students, "Here's another ancient epic you may want to read in your spare time."

CAST OF CHARACTERS

Note: The names of characters who are definitely female are in bold.

1. **CYNTHIA**: Goddess of the Moon and of Hunting. She is also called Diana. Her Greek name is Artemis. In Elizabethan drama, Cynthia is often allegorically Queen Elizabeth I. She does not drink from the Fountain of Self-Love.

2. MERCURY: God of Thieves. He disguises himself as a page and serves Hedon.

3. CUPID: God of Love. He disguises himself as a page and serves Philautia. Cupid can make people fall in love with each other who ought not to fall in love with each other.

4. HESPERUS: Personification of the Evening Star.

5. **ECHO**: former attendant of Juno, Queen of the Gods. Echo is a woman.

Echo fell in love with Narcissus, a beautiful mortal, but he saw his reflection in a pool of water and fell in love with it. Unable to move away from the sight of himself in the pool of water, he wasted away and died. After he died, a flower sprang up where he died. Echo also wasted away from grief until she became no more than her voice, which repeats the words that others say.

According to one myth, Juno took away Echo's voice because Echo helped Juno's husband, Jupiter, king of the gods, to hide his adulteries from her.

6. CRITICUS. The name means "critic." Good critics (as in the case of good satirists) are capable of pointing the way (and following the way) to moral improvement. Criticus is a wise scholar. He does not drink from the Fountain of Self-Love.

7. **ARETE**. The name means "Excellence" or "Virtue." Lady Arete is wise, excellent, and virtuous. She does not drink from the Fountain of Self-Love.

8. AMORPHUS. The name means "Shapeless" and "Misshapen" and "Deformed." Amorphus may be adaptable, and he may have a shifting nature and character. He is a foolish male courtier.

9. **PHANTASTE**. The name means "Fantasy," which can mean Self-Delusion. Phantaste has a Light Wittiness. Phantaste is a woman. She is a foolish female courtier. Courtiers are attendants at court. The word "light" can mean unimportant and trivial.

10. ASOTUS. The name means "Prodigal." The Prodigal engages the Beggar to be his attendant and serve him. Asotus is a foolish male courtier.

11. **ARGURION**. The name means "Silver," or "Money" since some money is silver. Argurion is a woman. She does not drink from the Fountain of Self-Love.

12. HEDON. The name means "Voluptuous," as in "Hedonistic." He is a hedonistic courtier. He is a foolish male courtier.

13. **PHILAUTIA**. The name means "Self-Love." Philautia is a court lady. She is a foolish female courtier.

14. ANAIDES. The name means "Shameless." He is an impudent courtier. He is a foolish male courtier.

15. **MORIA**. The name means "Folly." Moria is a woman. She is like a mother to some of the young unmarried women: She is the Mother of the Maidens. She is a foolish female courtier.

16. PROSAITES. The name means "Beggar." He is a boy. He is a foolish page.

17. COS. The name means "Whetstone." Liars were punished by being made to wear whetstones around their neck. He is a boy. He is a foolish page.

18. MORUS. The name means "Simpleton." He is a foolish page.

19. **GELAIA**. The name means "Laughter." Laughter is the daughter of Folly. In the play, Laughter is a young woman (a wench dressed in a page's clothing). She serves Anaides as a page. She is a foolish female courtier.

Note: In Ben Jonson's society, the word "wench" is not necessarily negative. It can be affectionate.

20. PHRONESIS *mute*. The name means "Prudence." She does not drink from the Fountain of Self-Love.

Note: The word "mute" means "a character who does not speak."

21. THAUMA *mute*. The name means "Wonder." She does not drink from the Fountain of Self-Love.

22. TIMÈ *mute*. The name means "Honor." She does not drink from the Fountain of Self-Love.

A TAILOR
FIRST CHILD
SECOND CHILD
THIRD CHILD

THE SCENE: GARGAPHIE

Gargaphie is a forested valley in Boeotia, Greece. It was sacred to Diana, goddess of the hunt. It is also the place where Actaeon was killed: See Ovid, *Metamorphoses* 3.155-156. In the play, it is spelled "Gargaphia" one time.

***

An archaic meaning of "fountain" is a spring of water that comes from the Earth and forms a pool of water. The surface of the pool can be still and form a natural mirror.

In Ben Jonson's society, a person of higher rank would use "thou," "thee," "thine," and "thy" when referring to a person of lower rank. (These terms were also used affectionately and between equals.) A person of lower rank would use "you" and "your" when referring to a person of higher rank.

"Sirrah" was a title used to address someone of a social rank inferior to the speaker. Friends, however, could use it to refer to each other.

The word "wench" at this time was not necessarily negative. It was often used affectionately.

A presence chamber is a reception room.

This play was first performed by a company of boy actors. In Ben Jonson's society, boys always played the parts of women.

Ben Jonson mostly uses the Roman names of the gods, but he sometimes uses the Greek names. Here are the names of some of the gods (Roman name first):

Apollo: Apollo

Cupid: Cupid

Diana: Artemis

Juno: Hera

Jupiter, aka Jove: Zeus

Latona: Leto

Mercury: Hermes

Minerva: Athena

Neptune: Poseidon

Vulcan: Hephaestus

Venus: Aphrodite

Artemis (also called Diana and Cynthia and some other names) and Apollo are twins. Their father is Jupiter, and their mother is Leto. In the form of a swan, Jupiter went to Leto and impregnated her.

***

Cynthia has many names: Diana: Artemis, Phoebe, etc.

One reason for this is that the Greeks and the Romans worshipped goddesses who were similar and so were conflated as one.

Another reason is that Cynthia was a tripartite goddess of the Moon, the Earth, and the Underworld.

• As a goddess of the Moon, she was known as Phoebe and as Luna and as Selene.

• As a goddess of the Earth, she was known as Artemis and as Diana.

• As a goddess of the Underworld, she was known as Hecate.

In slightly other words:

Cynthia is a tripartite goddess: a goddess with three forms.

• In Heaven, she is Luna, goddess of the Moon.

• On Earth, she is Diana (Roman name) and Artemis (Greek name), goddess of the hunt.

• In Hell, she is Hecate, goddess of witchcraft.

Cynthia was born on Mount Cynthus on the island of Delos.

In this play, Cynthia (derived from Mount *Cynthus*) is also sometimes called Delia (derived from the island of *Delos*).

Samuel Daniel wrote a sonnet cycle about a woman named Delia. The sonnet cycle, which is mentioned in *Cynthia's Revels*, can be found here:

http://www.luminarium.org/renascence-editions/delia.html

Artemis has many epithets or bynames. Delia is an epithet or byname for the goddess Artemis (Cynthia).

***

Myths frequently contradict other myths. They were told orally in many widely separated parts of Greece and Italy and other countries around the Mediterranean, and they changed in the retelling.

4

And so, according to various myths, the father of Cupid is Jupiter or Mercury or Mars. His mother, however, is always Venus.

AD LECTOREM

[To the Reader]

Nasutum volo, nolo polyposum.

The Latin is from Martial, *Epigrammata* 12.37.2.

An anonymous translator (Bohn's Classical Library (1897)) rendered the full epigram in this way:

You wish to be regarded as having an extremely good nose.

I like a man with a good nose, but object to one with a polypus.

https://topostext.org/work/677

"Polypus" is an archaic term for "polyp," which is a small growth protruding from the surface of a mucous membrane.

A person who is *nasutum* is a person who is more than ordinarily intelligent.

Ben Jonson is saying that he wants good audience members: people who can enjoy a good play without being biased against it without good reason.

PRELUDE

Three children entered the scene and began to argue over which of them would speak the Prologue to the play. All of them wanted to speak it because each child possessed Self-Love. The first child was wearing a cloak. The children were all boys.

"Please, you children, go away!" the first child said to the other two children. "Why, children? God's so, what do you mean?"

"God's so" is a variant of "catzo" or "cazzo," Italian slang for "penis." It may also or instead mean "By God's soul."

"By the Virgin Mary, we mean that you shall not speak the prologue, sir," the second child said.

"Why?" the third child asked. "Do you hope to speak it?"

"Aye, and I think I have the most right to speak it," the second child said. "I am sure I studied it first."

"That doesn't matter if the author of the play thinks I can speak it better," the third child said.

"I plead possession of the cloak," the first child said.

The person who spoke the Prologue at the beginning of plays customarily wore a cloak.

The first child said to the audience, "Ladies and gentlemen, give me your attention, for God's sake."

A voice from offstage said, "Why, children, aren't you ashamed? Come in there! Let the Prologue be performed!"

"By God's eyelid, I'll play nothing in the play, unless I speak the Prologue," the third child said.

"Why, will you stand to most voices of the gentlemen?" the first child suggested. "Let that decide it."

The first child wanted the audience to vote with their voices for whichever child they wanted to speak the Prologue.

"Oh, no, sir gallant!" the third child said. "You presume to have the start of us there, and that makes you offer so bountifully."

"No, I wish that I would be whipped if I had any such thought," the first child said. "Try it by lots, either of you."

"Indeed, I dare tempt my fortune in a greater venture than this," the second child said.

"Well said, resolute Jack," the third child said to the second child. "I am content, too, as long as we two draw first."

The third child said to the first child, "Make the cuts."

The cuts would be made in three straws to make two of equal length and the third of a different length.

The first child said, "But will you snatch my cloak while I am stooping to make the cuts?"

"No, we scorn treachery," the third child said.

"Which cut shall determine which of us speaks the Prologue?" the second child asked. "The shortest straw? Or the longest straw?"

"The shortest," the third child said.

The first child, holding three straws in his hand, said, "Agreed. Draw."

The two other children drew straws, leaving the third straw in the first child's hands.

"The shortest straw has come to the shortest child," the first child said. "Fortune was not altogether blind in this."

The first child was the shortest child; the first child had drawn the shortest straw and so was supposed to say the Prologue. The first child was also the child with the cloak.

Lady Fortune is usually thought to be blind.

"Now, children, I hope I shall go forward without your malicious envy," the first child said.

The first child wanted to speak the Prologue without being interfered with by the other children.

"Curses on all evil luck!" the second child said. "I touched the winning straw. I could have picked it."

"Wait, Jack," the third child said. "By God's eyelid, I'll do something now before I go in, although it be nothing but to revenge myself on the author, since I don't speak his Prologue. I'll tell all the argument — the plot — of his play beforehand, and so make stale his invention to the auditory — the audience — before the play begins."

"Oh, don't do that," the first child said.

"By no means," the second child said.

The third child began to tell you, the audience, the plot of the play, while the other two children interfered with and bothered him.

The third child said:

"First, the title of his play is *Cynthia's Revels*, as any man who has hope to be saved by his book can witness."

The title of the play was written on a banner above the stage. People who were literate could read the banner. They could also plead benefit of clergy if they were literate and so be tried in an ecclesiastical court rather than a civil court. Doing so could keep a person accused of a crime from being hung.

Also, a person who reads a satire and recognizes him- or herself in that satire can reform him- or herself and so be saved.

The third child continued:

"The scene is Gargaphia, which I do vehemently suspect to be some fustian country, but let that vanish."

One meaning of "fustian" is "imaginary."

The third child continued:

"Here is the court of Cynthia, whither Ben Jonson, our playwright, brings Cupid, travelling on foot, resolved to pretend to be a page: a boy servant.

"Along the way, Cupid meets with Mercury. (As that's a thing to be noted, take any of our playbooks without a Cupid or a Mercury in it and burn it for a heretic in poetry.)"

One of the boys pinched him.

The third child said to that boy, "Please, let me alone!"

He then continued:

"Mercury, in the nature of a conjurer, raises up Echo, who weeps over her love, or daffodil, Narcissus. She then sings a little and curses the spring wherein the pretty, foolish gentleman melted himself away, and there's an end of her."

A boy pinched him.

The third child continued:

"Now, I am to inform you that Cupid and Mercury both become pages in the play."

Pages are boy servants.

The third child continued:

"Cupid attends on and serves Philautia, or Self-Love, a court lady.

"Mercury follows and serves Hedon, the Voluptuous — Hedonistic — courtier, one who ranks himself even with Anaides, or the Impudent gallant (and that's my part), a fellow who keeps Laughter, the daughter of Folly (a wench in boy's attire) to wait on him."

The three boys would play parts in the forthcoming play. The third boy would play Anaides.

A boy pinched him.

The third child continued:

"These, in the court, meet with Amorphus, or the Deformed, a traveler who has drunk from the Fountain of Self-Love and there tells the wonders about the water; they immediately dispatch away their pages with bottles to fetch water from it, and themselves go to visit the ladies. But, I should have told you —"

The other boys were continuing to pinch the third child, who said, "Look, these emmets — that is, these ants, the other children — put me out here. They interfere with my speech."

The third child then continued with what he had been saying:

"— that with this Amorphus, there comes along a citizen's heir, Asotus, or the Prodigal, who, in imitation of the traveler who has the Whetstone following him, engages the Beggar to be his attendant."

The Whetstone is a page named Cos.

A boy pinched him.

The third child continued:

"Now, the nymphs who are mistresses to these gallants are Philautia (Self-Love), Phantaste (Fantasy, who has a Light Wittiness), Argurion (Money), and their guardian, Mother Moria (Mistress Folly)."

"I say to thee, say no more," the second child said, pinching him.

The third child continued:

"There Cupid strikes Money in love with the Prodigal, makes her dote upon him, give him jewels, bracelets, carcanets [necklaces or ornamental collars], etc., all of which he most ingeniously — naïvely — gives away, to be made known to the other ladies and gallants; and in the heat of this newfound wealth increases his train of servants with the Fool to follow him, as well as the Beggar."

In Ben Jonson's society, the word "ingenious" was sometimes used to mean "ingenuous," which can mean "well-born" or high-minded" or "innocent."

A boy pinched him.

The third child continued:

"By this time the Beggar has begun to wait in close attendance, and he has returned with the rest of his fellow bottle-men — servants who are in charge of bottles."

Bottle-men can be in charge of a wine cellar, and they can be servers of wine. These particular "bottle-men" bring back water in bottles.

A boy pinched him.

The third child continued:

"There they all drink, except for Argurion, who has fallen into a sudden apoplexy —"

"Stop his mouth!" the first child said, attempting to put his hand over the third child's mouth. The first child was worried that the third child would reveal too much of Ben Jonson's plot before the play even began.

The third child continued:

"And then there's a retired — that is, not in public life — Scholar there (you would not wish a thing to be better condemned and despised by a society of gallants than it — the Scholar — is), and he applies his service, good gentleman, to the Lady Arete, or Virtue, a poor nymph of Cynthia's train of attendants who is scarcely able to buy herself a gown; you shall see her play in a black robe soon. She is a creature who, I assure you, is no less scorned than the Scholar is."

Criticus is a wise critic and scholar.

Ben Jonson, a satirist, believed that his society often scorned scholarship and virtue.

The third child then asked:

"Where am I now? At a standstill?"

"Come, leave off at last yet," the second child said. "Stop talking."

The other children covered the eyes of the third child, who said:

"Oh, the night has come (it was somewhat dark, I thought) and Cynthia intends to come forth; that helps it a little yet."

Cynthia is goddess of the Moon; she would bring moonlight.

The third child continued:

"All of the courtiers must provide for revels; they decide upon a masque, the device of which is —"

A masque is an entertainment in which the performers wear masks. The masquers need not be professionals.

The third child said to the other two children, who were continuing to torment him, "What! Will you ravish — rape — me?"

The third child then continued with what he had been saying:

"— that each of these vices, being to appear before Cynthia, would seem other than indeed they are, and therefore assume and simulate the most neighboring virtues as their masquing costumes."

The third child said to the other two children, who were continuing to torment him, "I'd cry a rape except that you are children."

The second child said, "Come, we'll have no more of this anticipation. To give them the inventory of their cates — delicacies — beforehand is the custom of a tavern, and not befitting this company."

The first child said, "Tut, the purpose of all this exposition was but to show us the happiness of his memory. I thought at first he would have played the ignorant critic with everything along as he had gone. I expected some such trick."

"Oh, you shall see me do that splendidly," the third child said. "Lend me thy cloak."

"Be calm, sir," the first child said. "Do you intend to speak my prologue while wearing this cloak?"

"No, I wish that I might never stir from — leave — this place if I did," the third child said.

"Lend it to him," the second child said. "Lend it to him."

"Well, have you sworn that you will not speak the Prologue?" the first child asked.

"I have," the third child said.

The first child gave him the cloak.

The third child said:

"Now, sir, suppose that I am one of your gentlemanly auditors — audience members — who has come in, having paid my money at the door with much ado, and here I take my place and sit down.

"I have my three different kinds of tobacco in my pocket, my light by me, and thus I begin:

"By God's soul, I wonder that any man is so mad to come to see these rascally tits — that is, these rascally young men — play here."

He puffed on an imaginary pipe and continued:

"They do act like so many wrens or pismires [ants]" — he puffed — "not the fifth part of a good face among them all" — he puffed — "and then their music is abominable" — he puffed — "able to stretch and distress a man's ears worse than ten" — he puffed — "pillories, and their ditties" — he puffed — "are most lamentable things, like the pitiful fellows who make them" — he puffed — "poets."

Some people were punished by having their ears nailed to a pillory, which is a wooden frame with holes for restraining an offender's head and hands. The pillory was often mounted on a post.

The third child continued:

"By God's eyelid, if it weren't for tobacco" — he puffed — "I think" — he puffed — "the very stench of them would poison me. I would not dare to come in at their gates — a man would better visit fifteen jails" — he puffed — "or a dozen or two of hospitals — than once risk to come near them.

"How was my speech? Well?"

"Excellent," the first child said. "Give me my cloak."

"Wait!" the third child said. "You shall see me do another imitation now, but this time it will be of a more sober or better-composed gallant who is (as it may be thought) some friend or well-wisher to the house. And here I enter —"

"What!" the first child interrupted. "You'll step upon the stage, too?"

The second child said, "Yes, he will, and I step forth like one of the children and ask you, the gentleman: 'Would you have a stool, sir?'"

Gentlemen could rent a stool for sixpence and sit on the stage.

"A stool, boy?" the third child said.

"Aye, sir, if you'll give me sixpence, I'll fetch you one," the second child said.

"For what, I ask thee?" the third child said. "What shall I do with it?"

"Oh, God, sir!" the second child said. "Will you betray your ignorance so much? Why, you will enthrone yourself in state on the stage as other gentlemen are accustomed to do, sir."

"Away, wag!" the third child said. "What, would thou make an implement — a piece of furniture — out of me? By God's eyelid, the boy takes me for a piece of prospective, I hold my life, or some silk curtain come to hang on the stage here."

A perspective — not prospective — is a painted cloth that is used as a piece of stage background scenery.

The third child continued, "Sir Crack, I am none of your fresh pictures that are used to beautify the decayed dead arras — decorative cloth hangings — in a public theatre."

A "crack" is a cheeky child.

The second child said, "It is a sign, sir, that you don't put that confidence in your good clothes and your better face that a gentleman should do, sir. But I ask you, sir, to so let me be a suitor to you that you will quit our stage then and take a place. The play is soon to begin."

"Most willingly, my good wag," the third child said. "But I would speak with your author. Where is he?"

The author is Ben Jonson.

The second child said:

"He is not this way, I assure you, sir.

"We are not so officiously befriended by him as to have his presence in the tiring-house — dressing room — to prompt us aloud, stamp at the book-holder, aka prompter, swear for our properties, curse the poor tire-man, aka costumer, rail at the out-of-tune music, and sweat for every venial trespass we commit, as some authors would, if they had such fine ingles — favorite boys — as we.

"Well, it is just our hard fortune."

"Nay, Crack, don't be disheartened," the third child said.

"Not I, sir," the second child said. "But if you please to confer with our author by attorney — proxy — you may, sir; our proper self here stands for him."

The second child was offering to stand in the place of the playwright, Ben Jonson, and engage in conversation with the third child.

The third child said:

"Indeed, I have no such serious affair to negotiate with him, but what may very safely be turned upon thy trust.

"It is in the general behalf of this fair society here that I am to speak, at least the more judicious part of it, which seems much distasted with the immodest and obscene writing of many in their plays.

"Besides, they could wish that your poets would stop being promoters of other men's jests, and would waylay and ambush all the stale apophthegms — so-called witty sayings — or old books they can hear of, in print or otherwise, to farce — stuff — their scenes with."

Ben Jonson's preferred term for "playwright" was "poet."

The third child continued:

"They wish that your poets would not so penuriously glean wit from every laundress or hackney-man who lends horses for money, or derive their best grace with servile imitation from common stages, or observation of the company they converse with, as if their invention lived wholly upon another man's wooden dinner plate."

Ben Jonson's *Cynthia's Revels* was performed at Blackfriars, which was NOT a common stage.

The third child said:

"Again, that feeding their friends with nothing of their own, but what they have twice or thrice cooked, they should not wantonly give out how soon they had dressed — prepared — it; nor how many coaches came to carry away the broken meat — the leftovers — besides hobby-horses and foot-cloth-wearing nags."

Hobby-horses are small horses.

Footcloths were decorative pieces of cloth laid over the back of a horse.

In Ben Jonson's society, the word "nag" simply meant "horse" and not necessarily a bad horse.

The second child said, "So, sir, this is all the reformation you seek?"

The reformation requested was for originality in plays.

"It is," the third child said. "Don't you think it necessary to be practiced, my little wag?"

"Yes," the second child said, "where there is any such ill-habited custom received."

"Oh, I had almost forgotten it, too," the third child replied. "They say the *umbrae* or ghosts of some three or four plays departed a dozen years since have been seen walking on your stage here."

The accusation was that old plays were often performed on this stage.

The third child continued, "Take heed, boy. If your house is haunted with such hobgoblins, aka imps, it will frighten away all your spectators quickly."

The hobgoblins were old plays.

The second child said:

"Good, sir, but what will you say now if a poet, untouched with any breath of this disease, were to find God's tokens — signs of the bubonic plague — upon you who are of the audience?"

The second child mentioned some kinds of people who had been infected with this metaphorical bubonic plague:

"For example, a perfumed wit among you who knows no other learning than the price of satin and velvets, nor other perfection than the wearing of a neat suit, and yet will censure — judge to be good or bad — as desperately as the most professed critic in the house, presuming his clothes should bear him out in it.

"Another, whom it has pleased nature to furnish with more beard than brain, prunes — preens — his mustachio, lisps, and, with some score of affected oaths, swears down all who sit near him, 'that the old *Hieronimo,*' as it was first acted, 'was the only, best, and judiciously penned play of Europe.'"

Hieronimo is the major character in Thomas Kyd's play *The Spanish Tragedy.* This is one of the hobgoblins that the third child had criticized. Although popular, *The Spanish Tragedy* was old-fashioned.

The second child continued mentioning some kinds of people who had been infected with this metaphorical bubonic plague:

"A third great-bellied juggler — buffoon — talks of twenty years since and when Monsieur — Francis, Duke of Alençon — was here to court Queen Elizabeth, and he would enforce all wit to be of that fashion because his doublet — jacket — is still of that fashion.

"A fourth miscalls all by the name of 'fustian' that his grounded capacity cannot aspire to.

"A fifth only shakes his bottle-head, and out of his corky — frivolous — brain squeezes out a pitiful-learned face, and is silent."

People who are bottle-heads shake their heads. According to the cynical, they shake their heads in an attempt to hear whether anything is inside them.

The third child said, "By my faith, Jack, you have put me down. I wish I knew how to get off the stage with any reasonable grace. Here, take your cloak and promise some satisfaction in your prologue or, I'll be sworn, we have marred all."

The third child exited.

"Tut, fear not, Sall," the second child said to the first child.

"Sall" is short for the name "Salomon."

The second child continued:

"This will never offend the taste of a true sense. Don't forget your lines and do be good enough; I wish thou had some sugar that has been candied — crystallized — to sweeten thy mouth."

The second child exited.

PROLOGUE

Wearing the cloak, the first child said the Prologue:

"If gracious silence, sweet attention,

"Quick sight, and quicker apprehension

"(The lights of judgment's throne) shine anywhere,

"Our doubtful [uncertain whether the play will be a success] author [Ben Jonson] hopes this is their sphere [natural home].

"And therefore opens he himself to those;

"To other weaker beams his labors close,

"As loath to prostitute their virgin strain

"To every vulgar and adulterate [contaminated] brain.

"In this alone his muse her sweetness has:

"She shuns the print of any beaten path,

"And proves [tests] new ways to come to learned ears;

"Pied [Multi-colored, like the clothing of a Fool] ignorance she neither loves nor fears.

"Nor hunts she after popular applause,

"Or foamy [insubstantial] praise, that drops from common jaws;

"The garland that she wears, their hands must twine,

"Who can both censure [judge to be good or bad], understand, define

"What merit is. Then cast those piercing rays

"Round as a crown, instead of honored bays [wreath of laurel leaves],

"About his poesy; which, he knows, affords

"Words above action, matter above words."

***

The matter is the intellectual content of the play, which in this case is a satire. In this play, Ben Jonson is placing intellectual content above bombastic poetry and actions such as violent murders, both of which can be found in *The Spanish Tragedy*.

CHAPTER 1

— 1.1 —

Cupid and Mercury met each other.

"Who goes there?" Cupid asked.

"Blind archer, it is I," Mercury answered.

Cupid is often depicted as blindfolded. He shoots arrows that cause people to fall in love, but people often fall in love with the wrong or "wrong" person. Two boys may be very similar, but one boy may be rich and the other boy may be poor. A girl's father may wonder why she didn't fall in love with the rich boy instead of the poor boy.

"Who?" Cupid asked. "Mercury?"

"Aye," Mercury answered.

"Farewell," Cupid said.

"Stay, Cupid," Mercury requested.

"Not in your company, Hermes, unless your hands were riveted — handcuffed — at your back," Cupid replied.

Hermes (Mercury's Greek name) was the god of thieves. On the day that he was born, he stole 50 cattle from the god Apollo.

"Why so, my little rover?" Mercury replied.

A rover is 1) a person who wanders, aka roves, or 2) an arrow.

"Because I know you have not a finger but is as long as my quiver, cousin Mercury, when you please to extend it," Cupid answered.

Mercury used his long fingers to thieve. One thing that Cupid had to steal was his arrows.

In Ben Jonson's society, "cousin" and "cuz" meant "relative." The words could also mean "friend."

According to various myths, Cupid's father was either Mercury, or Mars, or Jupiter. His mother was Venus, goddess of beauty and sexual passion. Mars was the god of war, and Jupiter was the king of gods. Jupiter was the father of Mercury and Mars.

"Whence derive you this speech, boy?" Mercury asked. "Why do you say this?"

"Oh, it is your best policy to be ignorant," Cupid said.

He now mentioned some of Mercury's previous thefts:

"You did never steal Mars' sword out of the sheath, you? Nor Neptune's trident? Nor Apollo's bow? No, not you!

"Alas, your palms, Jupiter knows, are as tender as the foot of a foundered nag or a lady's face new mercuried; they'll touch nothing."

A foundered nag is a horse that is suffering from founder, a disease of the horse's foot.

Some women used mercury as a cosmetic. We now know that mercury is a poison. Ladies' facial skin could be irritated by the application of mercury, which can cause skin rashes and inflammation.

"Bah, infant, you'll be daring still," Mercury said.

Cupid said:

"Daring? Oh, Janus, what a word is there!"

Janus is a two-faced god.

Cupid continued:

"Why, my light feather-heeled" — Mercury wore feather-heeled sandals that made him fast — "coz, what are you any more than my uncle Jove's pander, aka pimp?"

Actually, Jove, aka Jupiter, is Mercury's father and Cupid's grandfather, but Ben Jonson's society used the words "uncle" and "cousin" loosely.

Jupiter had many, many affairs with goddesses and mortal women, and Mercury carried messages that facilitated these affairs.

Cupid continued:

"What are you any more than a lackey who runs on errands for him and can whisper a light message to a loose wench with some round — fluent — volubility, wait at a table with a trencher, and warble — play or sing while playing — upon a crowd a little?"

A crowd is a musical instrument similar to a viol.

Cupid continued:

"What are you any more than one who sweeps the gods' drinking room every morning, and sets the cushions in order again that they threw one at another's head overnight?

"That's the catalogue of all your employments now.

"Oh, no, I err.

"You have the marshalling of all the ghosts, too, that pass the Stygian ferry, and I suspect you for a share with the old sculler there, if the truth were known — but let that pass by and be ignored."

One of Mercury's duties as a god was to escort the souls of the dead to the Land of the Dead. He took them to the ferryman Charon, who ferried them across the Styx River to the Underworld.

Charon received money from the souls of the dead — corpses were buried with a coin on their eyes or in their mouths so they could pay the ferryman. Cupid is accusing Mercury of splitting the profits with Charon.

Scullers are rowers of sculls, aka small boats.

Cupid continued:

"You possess one other peculiar virtue in lifting — that is, thieving — or legerdemain, which few of the house of heaven have else besides, I must confess."

Legerdemain is sleight of hand, a good quality for a magician or a thief to have.

Cupid continued:

"But I think that should not make you set such an extreme distance between yourself and others, with the result that we should be said to over-dare in speaking to your nimble deity.

"So Hercules might challenge a priority of us both because he can throw the heavy bar farther or lift more joint-stools at the arm's end than we.

"If this might carry it, then we who have made the whole body of divinity tremble at the twang of our bow, and enforced Saturnius — Jupiter, a son of the god Saturn — himself to hide his curly haired forehead, thunder, and three-forked fires — lightning bolts — and put on a costume for masquing too light for a reveler of eighteen to be seen in —"

Jupiter could well tremble at the twang of Cupid's bow. Jupiter had a jealous wife, Juno, who hated his affairs.

Costumes for masques could be revealing.

Angry, Mercury interrupted, "— what is the meaning of this, my dancing braggart in decimo-sexto?"

A "decimo-sexto" is a small book; Cupid is still a boy.

The gods tend to be born and then grow to an age they will be at forever. Cupid is a boy forever, Mercury is a young man forever, and Jupiter is a mature man forever. A few gods or goddesses are already fully grown when they are born.

Mercury continued, "Charm your skipping tongue, or I'll —"

"What?" Cupid said. "You would use the virtue of your snaky tipstaff there upon us?"

Mercury carried a caduceus, a winged staff with two snakes wrapped around it.

Court officials carried a tipstaff.

These items were symbols of authority and could be used to hit someone such as Cupid.

Mercury said:

"No, boy, but I would use the stretched vigor of my arm about your ears."

He was threatening to box Cupid's ears with his fist.

Mercury continued:

"You have forgotten since the time when I took your heels up into air, on the very hour I was born, in sight of all the seated deities, when the silver roof of the Olympian palace rung again with the applause of the fact."

Cupid replied, "Oh, no, I remember it freshly and by a particular instance; for my mother Venus, at the same time, just stooped to embrace you, and — to speak by metaphor — you 'borrowed' a girdle of hers just as you 'borrowed' Jove's scepter, while he was laughing, and you would have 'borrowed' his thunder, too, except that it was too hot for your itching fingers."

"It is well, sir," Mercury said.

Cupid said:

"I heard you just looked in at Vulcan's forge the other day and 'entreated' a pair of his new tongs to go along with you for company."

Vulcan is the blacksmith god. According to the ancient Greek satirist Lucian, when Mercury was still a baby, he stole Vulcan's tongs and hid them in his baby clothes.

Cupid continued:

"It is joy on you, indeed, that you will keep your hooked talons in practice with anything.

"By God's light, now that you are on Earth, we shall have you filch spoons and candlesticks rather than fail.

"Pray Jove the perfumed courtiers keep their casting-bottles, toothpicks, and shuttlecocks away from you, or our more ordinary gallants their tobacco-boxes, for I am strangely jealous of your fingernails."

Casting-bottles are bottles for sprinkling perfumed water.

In Ben Jonson's society, toothpicks were fashionable items.

Mercury said:

"Never trust me again, Cupid, if you have not turned into a most acute gallant recently.

"The edge of my wit is completely taken off with the fine and subtle stroke of your thin-ground — eloquent — tongue; you fight with too poignant a phrase for me to deal with."

Cupid said, "Oh, Hermes, your craft cannot make me confident. I know my own steel — strength — to be almost spent, and therefore entreat my peace with you in time. You are too cunning for me to encounter at length, and I think it my safest ward to close."

Cupid was using a fencing metaphor. If he were to be very close to Mercury (Hermes) — within him, as within his arms — he would be safe from the thrusts of his sword.

"Well, for once I'll suffer you to come within me, wag," Mercury said, "but don't use these strains of speech too often, for they'll stretch my patience."

He then asked, "To where might you be marching now?"

Cupid answered:

"Indeed, to recover thy good thoughts, I'll reveal my whole plan and project.

"The huntress and queen of these groves, Diana, is aware of some black and envious slanders hourly breathed against her for her divine justice on Actaeon."

Cynthia, aka Diana, aka Artemis, is a virgin goddess who is militant about protecting her virginity as shown by the story of Actaeon:

Actaeon was out hunting with his dogs, and he saw the virgin goddess bathing naked. She turned him into a stag, and his own dogs ran him down and killed him. He suffered horribly because his mind was still human although his body was that of a male deer.

Cupid continued:

"Therefore, as she asserts, she has here in the valley of Gargaphie proclaimed ceremonial revels that she will grace with the full and royal expense of one of her clearest moons — the Moon will be bright.

"In this time of revels, it shall be lawful for all sorts of ingenuous — spirited — persons to visit her palace, to court her nymphs, to exercise all variety of generous and noble pastimes, as well to intimate how far she treads such malicious imputations beneath her, as also to show how clear her beauties are from the least wrinkle of austerity they may be charged with."

"But what is all this to you, Cupid?" Mercury asked.

Cupid answered, "Here I mean to put off the title of a god and take the clothing of a page, in which disguise, during the interim of these revels, I will get to follow some one of Diana's maids, where, if my bow hold and my shafts fly but with half the willingness and aim they are directed, I doubt not but I shall really — and royally — redeem the minutes I have lost by their so long and over-nice — overly fastidious — proscription of my deity from their court."

Diana/Cynthia was a virgin goddess, and her attendants were virgins, but on this night, Cupid had a chance to woo and pursue her attendants.

Normally, Cupid was banned from Diana's court. It's not good to have the god of love around attendants who are supposed to stay virgins.

Cupid was hoping to make one of Diana's virgin attendants a former virgin.

"Pursue it, divine Cupid," Mercury said. "It will be splendid!"

The gods frequently had affairs with goddesses, with mortal women and with nymphs, who were long-lived and almost immortal.

"But will Hermes second me and back me up?" Cupid asked.

Hermes/Mercury answered, "I am now to put in action and carry out a special assignment from my father Jove, but once that has been performed, I am ready for any fresh action that offers itself."

"Well, then we part," Cupid said.

He exited.

Alone, Mercury said to himself:

"Farewell, good wag. Now to my charge."

He called:

"Echo, fair Echo, speak! It is Mercury who calls thee. Sorrowful nymph, salute me with thy repercussive — echoing — voice, so that I may know what cavern of the Earth contains thy airy spirit; and so that I may know how or where I may direct my speech so that thou may hear me."

Echo, a voice underneath the stage, echoed Mercury's last word: "Here."

"So nigh?" Mercury said.

"Aye," Echo echoed.

Mercury said:

"Know, gentle soul, then, I am sent from Jove, who, pitying the sad burden of thy woes still growing on thee, in thy lack of words to vent thy passion — strong emotion — for Narcissus' death, commands that now, after three thousand years that have been exercised in Juno's spite, thou will take on a corporal figure and ascend, enriched with vocal and articulate power.

"Make haste, sad nymph. Thrice does my winged rod —my caduceus — strike the obsequious Earth to give thee way.

"Arise, and speak thy sorrows! Echo, rise."

Echo ascended from below the stage. Mercury, by the command of Jupiter, had given her a corporeal body and the ability to speak her own thoughts in her own words rather than merely repeating the words of others.

Three thousand years earlier, Echo had fallen in love with Narcissus, a beautiful mortal, but he saw his reflection in a pool of water and fell in love with it. Unable to move away from the sight of himself in the pool of water, he wasted away and died. After he died, a flower sprang up where he died. Echo also wasted away from grief until she became no more than her voice, which repeated the words that others said.

According to one myth, Juno took away Echo's voice because Echo helped Juno's husband, Jupiter, king of the gods, to hide his adulteries from her.

Mercury said, "We are here by this fountain where thy love did pine, whose memory lives fresh to vulgar — commonly known — fame, enshrined in this yellow flower that bears his name."

Daffodils are yellow flowers of the genus Narcissus.

Echo said:

"His name revives and lifts me up from Earth. Oh, which way shall I first convert — turn — myself, or in what mood shall I assay to speak, so that in a moment I may be delivered of the prodigious grief I go with?

"See, see, the mourning fountain whose spring weeps yet the untimely fate of that too beauteous boy, that trophy of Self-Love and spoil of nature, who, now transformed into this drooping flower, hangs the repentant head back from the stream as if it wished, 'I wish that I had never looked in such a flattering mirror.'

"Oh, Narcissus, thou who were once, and yet are, my Narcissus, had Echo but been privy to and known thy thoughts, she would have dropped away herself in tears until she had turned into all water, so that in her, as in a truer mirror, thou might have gazed and seen thy beauties by a kinder reflection.

"But Self-Love never yet could look on truth except with bleared beams — blurred eyesight; sleek Flattery and Self-Love are twin-born sisters, and they so mix their eyes — look into each other's eyes and unite their souls — so that if you sever one, the other dies."

If you take away Self-Love, Flattery dies (the person will cease to flatter him- or herself); and if you take away Flattery, Self-Love dies.

Self-Love and Flattery are very close: They are as close as twins.

Echo continued:

"Why did the gods give thee a heavenly form and earthy thoughts to make thee proud of it?

"Why do I ask? It is now the known disease that beauty has, to bear too deep a sense of her own self-conceived excellence.

"Oh, had thou known the worth of heaven's rich gift, thou would have turned it to a truer use."

A truer use of beauty is to attract a mate with whom one can reproduce.

Echo continued:

"And not, with lean and covetous ignorance, pined in continual eyeing that bright gem, the glance whereof to others had been more than to thy famished mind the wide world's store."

To Narcissus, his beauty was worth the entire world.

To others such as Echo, Narcissus' beauty was worth more than the entire world. It was worth the entire world plus the baby that would be born to Narcissus and his wife (whom Echo would have liked to be).

Echo continued:

"So wretched is it to be merely rich."

Narcissus was rich in beauty, but he could have been rich both in beauty and in children.

Echo concluded:

"Witness thy youth's dear sweets here spent untasted,

"Like a fair taper — candle — with his — its — own flame wasted."

Mercury said, "Echo, be brief; Saturnia is abroad, and if she hears you, she'll storm at Jove's high will."

"Saturnia" means "daughter of Saturn." Here it means in particular Juno, the wife of Jupiter. Yes, they are brother and sister as well as husband and wife.

If Juno hears Echo, Juno will be angry at Jupiter because he has restored her voice, at least temporarily. Yes, even after three thousand years, Juno still wants to punish Echo.

Echo replied:

"I will, kind Mercury, be brief as time."

Time can be brief or long. Here, it means the time needed, which is brief.

Echo continued:

"Allow me to do him these last rites: Just to kiss his flower and sing some mourning strain — song — over his watery hearse."

An obsolete meaning of "hearse" is "tomb."

Mercury said:

"Thou do obtain thy wish. I would be no son to Jove if I were to deny thee.

"Begin, and more to grace thy cunning voice, the humorous air shall mix her solemn tunes with thy sad words.

"Strike, Music, from the spheres,

"And with your golden raptures swell our ears."

"Humorous" here means "filled with humors," aka moods.

At one time, people thought that the planets and the Sun and the stars were encased in crystalline spheres that revolved around the Earth.

The music of the spheres was thought to be beautiful.

Music played.

Echo said:

"Slow, slow, fresh fountain, keep time with my salt tears. Yet, slower, yet, O faintly gentle springs. Listen to the heavy part the music bears.

"Woe weeps out her division — her melody — when she sings."

Echo sang:

"Droop herbs, and flowers,
"Fall grief in showers;
"Our beauties are not ours.
"Oh, I could still,
"Like melting snow upon some craggy hill,
"Drop, drop, drop, drop,
"Since nature's pride is now a withered daffodil."

Mercury said, "Now, have you finished?"

Echo said, "I will be finished soon, good Hermes; be patient a little while. Allow my thirsty eye to gaze a little while, just even to taste the place, and I am vanished."

Mercury replied, "Forgo thy use and liberty of tongue — thy freedom of speech — and thou may dwell on Earth and entertain thee there."

If Echo would refrain from freely speaking and criticizing the gods, she could dwell again on Earth in bodily form and with her voice. If she would not refrain from freely speaking and criticizing the gods, her voice would become an echo again and she would live in caves without a bodily form.

Echo criticized some of Cynthia's actions:

"Here young Actaeon fell, pursued and torn by Cynthia's wrath, more eager than his hounds.

"And here — woe is me, the place is deadly — see the weeping Niobe transported hither from Phrygian mountains, and by Phoebe reared as the proud trophy of her sharp revenge."

Niobe was proud. She had given birth to six sons and six daughters, and she boasted aloud, "I am more worthy of respect than the goddess Leto, who has given birth to only two children: the twins Apollo and Artemis." Leto's children were angry at the disrespect shown to their mother, and with the anger of the gods, they killed all of Niobe's children in one day by shooting them with arrows. Because of Niobe's pride, Apollo and Diana turned her to stone. Even when she was stone, she grieved for the deaths of her children, and tears trickled down her marble cheeks. Niobe was so proud that she thought she was a better mother than the goddess mother of the god Apollo and goddess Diana.

Phoebe, Diana, and Artemis are other names for Cynthia. Cynthia was a virgin goddess; she was also a tripartite goddess, and as Phoebe (and as Luna) she was the goddess of the Moon.

Mercury said, "Nay, but listen —"

Echo interrupted, "But here, oh, here, is the Fountain of Self-Love in which Latona and her careless — without cares, and uncaring — nymphs, regardless of my sorrows, bathe themselves in hourly pleasures."

Latona is the Roman name of Leto, the mother of Cynthia.

Possibly, "Latona" should be "Latonia," or "daughter of Latona." In that case, "Latonia" would be Cynthia.

Mercury said:

"Stop thy babbling tongue, fond — foolish and doting — Echo. Thou profane the grace that is done to thee. Similarly idle worldlings — worldly minded people — merely made of voice, censure and judge the powers above them.

"Come away!

"Jove calls thee from here away and his will brooks — tolerates — no stay."

Echo said:

"Oh, stay! Wait!

"I have just one poor thought to clothe in airy garments and speak out loud, and then, indeed, I will go."

She cursed the fountain:

"Henceforth, thou treacherous and murdering spring, be forever called the Fountain of Self-Love; and with thy water let this curse remain as a plague that cannot be separated from the water:

"My curse is that any person who tastes even a drop thereof may with the instant touch grow dotingly enamored on themselves.

"Now, Hermes, I have finished."

Mercury (Hermes) replied:

"Then thy speech must here forsake thee, Echo, and thy voice, as it was accustomed to do, will rebound but the last words someone speaks to you.

"Farewell."

"Well," Echo echoed.

She meant that she understood what he had told her about losing her freedom of speech. She had used her freedom of speech to criticize the gods, and now her voice would again become an echo.

She began to descend into the Earth again.

Mercury said:

"Now, Cupid, I am for you and your mirth
"To make me light and happy before I leave the Earth."

Amorphus entered the scene and saw Echo.

The word "amorphous" means "shapeless."

Amorphus said to Echo, "Dear spark of beauty, don't go so fast away!"

"Away!" Echo echoed.

Seeing this, Mercury said to himself, "Wait, let me observe this portent still."

Amorphus said to Echo, "I am neither your minotaur, nor your centaur, nor your satyr, nor your hyena, nor your baboon, but just a traveler, believe me."

The Minotaur is a half-human, half-bull monster.

Centaurs are half-human and half-horse.

Satyrs are woodland gods, half-human and half-goat.

"Leave me," Echo echoed.

Unimpressed with Amorphus, Mercury said to himself, "I guessed it should be some travelling motion — puppet — who pursued Echo so."

Amorphus asked Echo, "Do you know from whom you flee, or whence?"

"Hence!" Echo echoed.

She exited.

Thinking himself alone, Amorphus said to himself, "This is somewhat above strange: a nymph of her feature and lineament to be so preposterously rude. Well, I will just cool myself at yonder spring and then follow her."

Mercury said to himself, "Nay, then, I am familiar with the issue: I know how things will turn out. I'll leave you, too."

How will things turn out? Amorphus will drink the cursed water.

Mercury exited.

Now alone, Amorphus said to himself:

"I am a rhinoceros if I had thought a creature of her symmetry would have dared so improportionable — out of proportion — and abrupt a digression — an exit.

"Liberal and divine fountain, allow my profane hand to partake of thy bounties."

He drank water from the fountain.

He then said to himself:

"By the purity of my taste, here is most ambrosiac water. I will sup of it again.

"With thy permission, sweet fountain."

Ambrosia is the food of the gods.

He drank again.

Filled with Self-Love, Amorphus said to himself:

"See, the water, a more running, subtle, and humorous nymph than she [Echo], permits me to touch and handle her.

"What should I infer from this rejection?

"If my behaviors had been of a cheap or customary garb, my accent or phrase vulgar, my garments trite [frayed], my countenance illiterate or unpracticed in the encounter of a beautiful and brave-attired piece [splendidly dressed woman], then I might, with some change of color, have suspected my faculties and abilities.

"But knowing myself to be an essence so sublimated and refined by travel, of so studied and well-exercised a gesture, so alone and unequaled in fashion, able to make — imitate — the face of any statesman living, and to speak the mere extraction — that is, the finest essence — of language; and one who has now made the sixth return upon venture —"

Amorphus was a traveler and a gambler. He made bets that he could travel to and from a certain place within an allotted time. He had won six such bets.

He continued:

"— and was the first who ever enriched his country with the true laws of the *duello* [duel]; whose optics — eyes — have drunk the spirit of beauty in some eight score and eighteen princes' courts, where I have resided, and been there fortunate in the amours of three hundred forty and five ladies, all nobly descended, whose names I have in catalogue; to conclude, in all so happy as even admiration herself does seem to fasten her kisses upon me.

"Certainly I do neither see, nor feel, nor taste, nor savor the least smell, steam, or fume of a reason that should invite this foolish, fastidious nymph so peevishly to abandon me.

"Well, let the memory of her fleet — fly — into air; my thoughts and I are for this other element: water."

Criticus and Asotus entered the scene. Criticus was a man of good judgment; Asotus was a man of prodigality.

"What?" Criticus said. "The well-dieted Amorphus has become a water-drinker? I see he does not intend to write verses then."

Some people believe that alcohol is a source of poetic inspiration.

"No, Criticus?" Amorphus said. "Why?"

Criticus replied, "*Quia nulla placere diu, nec vivere carmina possunt, quae scribuntur aquae potoribus.*"

The Latin quotation (with *Quia* added to it), which is from Horace's *Epistles* 1.192-3, means "Because no songs that have been written by drinkers of water can please or live on for a long time."

"What do you say to your Helicon?" Amorphus asked.

Helicon is a mountain in Boeotia that is the source of a spring sacred to the Muses. Drinking its water was thought to cause poetic inspiration.

"Oh, the Muses' well!" Criticus said. "That's always excepted."

"Sir, the Muses have no such water as the water in this fountain, I assure you," Amorphus said. "Neither nectar nor the juice of nepenthe is anything compared to it. It is better than metheglin, believe it!"

Nectar is the drink of the gods.

Nepenthe is a drug mentioned in Homer's *Odyssey*; the drug banishes worry.

Metheglin is a Welsh spiced drink.

"Metheglin!" Asotus said. "What's that, sir, may I be so audacious to demand?"

"A kind of Greek wine I have met with, sir, in my travels," Amorphus answered. "It is the same that Athenian orator Demosthenes usually drank in the composure — the composition — of all his exquisite and mellifluous orations."

Criticus said, "That's to be argued, Amorphus, if we may credit Lucian, who in his *Encomium Demosthenis — Praise of Demosthenes —* affirms that Demosthenes never drank anything but water in any of his composition sessions."

"Lucian is absurd; he knew nothing," Amorphus said. "I will believe my own travels before all the Lucians of Europe. He feeds you with fictions and leasings."

Leasings are lies.

Indeed, Lucian wrote a book about travelling to the Moon.

"Indeed, I think, next to a traveler, he does prettily well," Criticus said.

"I assure you that it was wine," Amorphus said. "I have tasted it, and from the hand of an Italian antiquary who derives it — traces its genealogy — authentically from the Duke of Ferrara's bottles."

The Duke of Ferrara was a patron of the arts.

Amorphus then asked, "What is the name of the gentleman you are in rank with there, sir?"

"He is Asotus, son to the late deceased Philargyrus the citizen," Criticus answered.

Philargyrus is derived from the Greek word for "money-lover."

"Was his father of any eminent place or means?" Amorphus asked.

"He was to have been praetor next year," Criticus answered.

The office of Praetor was the second highest political office of the Roman Republic. Praetors were subject only to the veto of the Consuls. Among other duties, Praetors could take the auspices, the performance of which was a religious rite.

The location, however, was Greece, and "praetor" meant a high administrative office, such as mayor or chief magistrate.

Amorphus said:

"Ha! He's a pretty formal — shapely — young gallant, truly. It's a pity he is not more genteelly propagated — better born.

"Listen, Criticus; you may say to him who I am, if you please. Although I do not affect — desire — popularity, yet I would be loath to stand out to — that is, spurn — anyone whom you shall grant to call your friend."

"Sir, I fear I may do wrong to your sufficiencies — abilities — in the reporting them by forgetting or misplacing some one of them," Criticus replied. "You can best inform him about yourself, sir, unless you have some catalogue or inventory of your faculties ready-drawn that you would request me to show him for you, and for him to take notice of."

Realizing that Criticus did not want to praise him to Asotus, Amorphus said to himself, "This Criticus is sour."

He then said out loud, "I will think, sir."

He would think about the best way to get to know Asotus.

"Do so, sir," Criticus said.

He then said to himself, "Oh, heaven, that anything in the likeness of man should endure these racked extremities for the uttering of his sophisticate — adulterated — good parts!"

Asotus then took Criticus aside and said to him quietly, "Criticus, I have a request to make to you, but you must not deny me. Please make this gentleman and me friends."

Criticus said, "Friends! Why? Is there any difference between you? Have you quarreled?"

"No," Asotus said. "I mean make us acquaintances: for us to know one another."

"Oh, now I understand you," Criticus said. "I did not understand your meaning before."

Actually, Criticus was leery of introducing the two men for fear that Amorphus would take advantage of Asotus, the young prodigal.

Asotus said, "In good faith, he's a most excellent rare — splendid — man, I am sure."

Criticus said to himself, "By God's light, they are mutually enamored by this time."

"Will you, sweet Criticus?" Asotus pleaded.

"Yes, yes," Criticus replied.

"Nay, but when?" Asotus said. "You'll defer it now and forget it?"

"Why, is it a thing of such immediate necessity that it requires so violent and quick a dispatch?" Criticus asked.

"No, but — I wish I might never stir — he's a most ravishing man," Asotus said. "Good Criticus, you shall endear me to you indeed, I say!"

"Well, your longing shall be satisfied, sir," Criticus said.

"And in addition you may tell him who my father was, and how well-off he left me, and that I am his heir," Asotus said.

"Leave it to me, I'll forget none of your dear graces, I assure you," Criticus said.

"Nay, I know you can better marshal these affairs than I can," Asotus replied.

He then said to himself, "O gods, I'd give all the world, if I had it, for an abundance of such acquaintances."

Criticus said to himself, "What ridiculous circumstance might I devise now to bestow this reciprocal brace — pair — of coxcombs — fools — one upon another?"

They were reciprocal because each wished to be introduced to the other.

Thinking of a way to get to know Asotus, Amorphus said to himself:

"Since I trod on this side of the Alps, I was not so frozen in my invention.

"Let me see, to accost him with some choice remnant of Spanish, or Italian would indifferently express my languages now."

"Indifferently" can mean 1) "casually," or 2) "poorly."

Amorphus continued speaking to himself:

"By the Virgin Mary, then, if Asotus would turn out to be ignorant, it would be both hard and harsh on him.

"How else can I get to know him?

"Step into some discourse of state — politics — and so make my introduction? That would be above him, too, and out of his element, I fear.

"Pretend to have seen him in Venice or Padua, or some face near his in similitude? It is too pointed and open.

"No, it must be a more quaint and collateral — indirect — device as — wait: to frame some encomiastic — praising — speech upon this our metropolis, or the wise magistrates thereof, in which politic — wise — number it is likely that his father filled up a room?

"Descend into a particular admiration of their justice, for the due measuring of coals, burning of cans, and such like?"

Weights and measures are an important part of a magistrate's duties. "Cans" are wooden drinking vessels, and a magistrate would make a burn mark on the vessel to show what is a full measure.

Amorphus continued speaking to himself:

"Or also to praise their religion in pulling down a superstitious cross and advancing a Venus or Priapus in place of it?"

In Ben Jonson's London, crosses were removed because people thought they were Catholic. In the city of this play, statues of Venus and Priapus are put up in place of crosses.

Venus is the goddess of sexual passion, and Priapus, statues of whom displayed a giant phallus, was the god of fertility.

Amorphus continued speaking to himself:

"Ha! It will do well!

"Or to talk of some hospital whose walls record his father as a benefactor, or of so many emergency buckets for getting water to put out fires bestowed on his parish church in his lifetime, with his name at length, for lack of a coat of arms, tricked upon them? Any of these?

"Or to praise the cleanness of the street wherein he dwelt, or the provident painting of his posts in preparation for the time he should have been praetor."

Officials often began their careers by being responsible for the cleaning of streets.

Mayoral proclamations were placed on posts.

Amorphus continued speaking to himself:

"Or, leaving aside his parent, come to some special ornament about himself, such as his rapier, or some other of his accoutrements?

"I have it! Thanks, gracious Minerva."

Minerva is the Roman goddess of wisdom. Her Greek name is Athena.

Asotus said to himself, "I wish I had just at once spoken to him [Amorphus], and then —"

Amorphus then praised the collar that Asotus was wearing as a means of becoming introduced to him:

"It is a most curious and neatly wrought neckband, this same, as I have seen, sir."

"Oh, God, sir," Asotus said.

"Oh, God, sir" was a fashionable expression of little meaning.

"You forgive the humor of my eye in observing it?" Amorphus asked.

"Humor" was a fashionable word of many meanings and often of little meaning.

"Oh, Lord, sir, no such apology is needed, I assure you," Asotus said.

Criticus said to himself, "I am anticipated. They'll make a solemn deed of gift of themselves, you shall see."

"Your rose, too, suits you most gracefully, indeed," Amorphus said.

The rose was an ornamental ribbon worn on shoes.

"It is the most genteel and received wear now, sir," Asotus said.

Amorphus said, "Believe me, sir — I speak it not to humor you — I have not seen a young gentleman, generally, put on his clothes with more judgment."

Asotus was well and fashionably dressed.

"Oh, it is your pleasure to say so, sir," Asotus said.

"No, I swear as I am virtuous, being altogether untraveled, it strikes me into wonder," Amorphus said.

"Being altogether untraveled" was badly expressed; the phrase referred to Asotus, not to Amorphus, who was well traveled, according to his previous statements.

"I do purpose to travel, sir, at spring," Asotus said.

"I think I shall affect and take a liking to you, sir," Amorphus said. "This last speech of yours has begun to make you dear to me."

"Oh, God, sir, I wish there were anything in me, sir, that might appear worthy the least worthiness of your worth, sir," Asotus said. "I avow, sir, that I should endeavor to show it, sir, with more than common regard, sir."

Criticus said to himself, "Oh, here's excellent motley, sir."

Fools, aka jesters, wore motley: multi-colored clothing.

Amorphus said:

"Both your desert — merit — and your endeavors are plentiful. Do not suspect them.

"But your sweet disposition to travel, I assure you, has made you another myself — an alter ego — in my eye, and struck me enamored on your beauties."

Amorphus and Asotus were forming a mutual admiration society, one that had begun at first sight.

"I wish I were the fairest lady of France for your sake, sir, and yet I would travel, too," Asotus said.

Amorphus said, "Oh, you should digress from yourself else, for, believe it, travel is the only thing that rectifies or, as the Italian says, *vi rendi pronto all' attioni*."

He translated the Italian: "makes you fit for action."

"I think it is a great expense, though, sir," Asotus said.

Amorphus said:

"Expense? Why, it is nothing for a gentleman who goes private — alone — as yourself, or so; my intelligence shall cover my expenses at all times."

Amorphus lived by his wits. He found ways for other people to pay his expenses.

He then said:

"By my good faith, I swear this hat has possessed my eye exceedingly: It is so pretty and fantastic.

"What! Is it a beaver hat?"

A beaver hat is an expensive hat made out of beaver fur.

"Aye, sir. I'll assure you it is a beaver hat," Asotus said. "It cost me six crowns just this morning."

"A very pretty fashion, believe me, and a most novel kind of trim," Amorphus said. "Your button is conceited — cleverly designed — too!"

The button may have been an ornament on the hat.

"Sir, it is all at your service," Asotus said.

"Oh, pardon me," Amorphus said.

"I beseech you, sir, if you please to wear it, you shall do me a most infinite favor," Asotus said.

He wanted to give his expensive beaver hat to Amorphus.

Criticus said to himself, "By God's light, will he be praised out of his clothes?"

"By heaven, sir, I do not offer it to you after the Italian manner," Asotus said. "I wish you would believe that of me."

The Italian manner was to offer someone something but with the expectation that the gift will be declined.

The people who defined "the Italian manner" in this way were not Italian.

Amorphus replied:

"Sir, I shall fear to appear rude in denying your courtesies, especially being invited by so proper a distinction between the Italian manner and your manner.

"May I please ask for your name, sir?"

"My name is Asotus, sir."

Amorphus replied:

"I take your love, gentle Asotus, but let me persuade you to receive this in exchange —"

They exchanged hats, and Criticus said to himself, "By God's heart, they'll exchange doublets — jackets — soon."

Amorphus continued:

"— and from this time esteem yourself in the first rank of those few whom I profess to love.

"Why are you in the company of this scholar here? I will make you known to gallants such as Anaides the courtier, Hedon the courtier, and others whose society shall render you graced and respected.

"This scholar is a trivial fellow, too mean, too coarse for you to converse with."

Examining Amorphus' hat, Asotus said, "By God's eyelid, this hat is not worth a crown, and my hat cost me six crowns just this morning!"

Criticus said, "I looked for the time when Asotus would repent this exchange; he has begun to be sad for a good while."

Amorphus said:

"Sir, shall I say to you about that hat — be not so sad, be not so sad — that it is a relic I could not so easily have departed with, except as the hieroglyphic — the sign — of my affection.

"You shall alter it to what form you please; it will take any block. I have varied it myself to the three thousandth time, and not so few."

A block was a wooden mold for a hat. From it we derive the insult "blockhead."

Since he had varied its shape for the three thousandth time, it was a well-worn hat.

Amorphus continued:

"It has these virtues beside: Your head shall not ache under it, nor your brain leave you without permission; it will preserve your complexion to eternity, for no beam of the Sun, should you wear it under *zona torrida* — the torrid zone, aka tropics — has the force to approach it by two ells; it is proof against thunder and enchantment."

An ell is a unit of measurement.

Amorphus was claiming that his hat was made of a material that would repel lightning; such materials supposedly included hawthorn, laurel, and seal-skin.

Amorphus continued:

"And it was given to me by a great man in Russia as an especially prized present; and constantly affirmed to be the hat that accompanied the politic — crafty — Ulysses in his tedious and ten years' travels.

Ulysses is also known by his Greek name: Odysseus. He is one of the heroes of Homer's *Iliad* and the main hero of Homer's *Odyssey*. He left his home island of Ithaca, went to Troy, and fought until the Greeks conquered Troy, and then it took him another ten years of trouble to return home.

Once back on his home island of Ithaca, he discovered that his palace had been taken over by suitors who mistreated his wife and son. In order to stay alive until he could find a way to kill the suitors, he pretended to be a beggar.

Asotus said, "By Jove, I will not depart with this hat, no matter who would give me a million crowns for it."

Cos and Prosaites entered the scene.

The name "Prosaites" means "Beggar."

The name "Cos" means "Whetstone."

Looking for employment, Cos said, "May God save you, sweet bloods — young gentlemen. Do any of you want a creature or a dependent?"

Criticus said to himself, "Curse me, he's a fine blunt slave."

A creature is someone's creation: Give someone a job as a servant, and he is your creature. He is also your dependent: You will feed him.

In this context, a slave is a beggar.

Amorphus said to himself, "A page of good timber: He is well built. It will now be my grace to entertain him first, though I cashier — dismiss — him again in private."

Amorphus wanted to impress Asotus by hiring a servant.

He asked, "What are thou called?"

"Cos, sir, Cos."

Criticus said to himself, "Cos? How happily has Fortune furnished him — Amorphus — with a whetstone!"

In Ben Jonson's society, liars were punished by having a whetstone hung around their neck while they were in a pillory. Amorphus was a traveler, and travelers were known for telling lies about their travels.

Amorphus said:

"I do entertain you, Cos."

This kind of "entertain" means "hire."

Amorphus quietly added:

"Conceal your quality — your character — until we are private."

He was worried that Cos' character may be bad; after all, "Cos" meant "whetstone" and whetstones were hung around the necks of liars as punishment. In addition, he had hired him without an interview, simply in order to impress Asotus by hiring someone to be his page.

Amorphus continued quietly:

"If your parts are — that is, your character is — worthy of me, I will countenance — support — you; if not, I will catechize you."

A catechism is a set of religious questions and answers about Christian principles.

He then said out loud, "Gentlemen, shall we go?"

"Wait, sir," Asotus said, "I'll just entertain — hire — this other fellow and then —"

He said quietly to himself, "I have a great humor — desire — to taste of this water, too, but I'll come again alone for that."

The word "taste" can mean "touch." Asotus is usually generous, so he would be willing to share and drink the water with other people. He may have meant that he would come back later to bathe in the water.

Asotus continued out loud from where he had left off, "— mark the place."

He then asked, "What's your name, youth?"

"Prosaites, sir."

"Prosaites?" Asotus said. "A very fine name, Criticus, isn't it?"

"Yes, and a very ancient name, sir," Criticus said. "It means 'the beggar.'"

"Follow me, good Prosaites," Asotus said. "Let's talk."

Asotus, Prosaites, Cos, and Amorphus exited.

Alone now, Criticus said to himself:

"He will rank even with you before long if you hold on to your course."

The prodigal — Asotus — would soon be like the beggar — Prosaites — if he continued wasting his money.

Criticus continued:

"O Vanity, how are thy painted beauties doted on by light and empty idiots!"

People in this society called makeup "paint." In this context, "painted" was metaphorical as well as literal.

Criticus continued:

"How pursued with open and extended appetite and eagerness!

"How they sweat and run themselves out of breath, raised on their toes, to catch thy airy forms, always turning giddy until they reel like drunkards who buy the merry madness of one hour with the long irksomeness of following time!"

Drunk people pay for the happiness of one alcoholic hour with a long hangover the next day.

"Oh, how despised and base a thing is man if he does not strive to erect his groveling — face-down — thoughts above the strain of flesh!

"But how much cheaper he is when even his best and understanding part, the crown and strength of all his faculties, floats like a dead drowned body on the stream of vulgar humor mixed with the commonest dregs!"

The word "humor" has many meanings, including "fluid." Much more often, it means "mood" or "fashion."

Criticus continued:

"I suffer for their guilt now, and my soul, like one who looks on ill-affected — diseased — eyes, is hurt with mere intention — simply gazing — on their follies.

"Why will I view them then, my sense might ask me?

"Is it either a rarity, or some new object, that strains my strict observance to this point?

"Oh, I wish it were, therein I could afford that my spirit should draw a little near to theirs to gaze on novelties, so long as Vice were a novelty."

Criticus is disgusted because he is watching the fools. If vice were a novelty, he might forgive himself a little for watching this display of vice. But he, like most or all of us, has seen lots of vice and so vice is no novelty.

Criticus continued:

"Tut, she — Vice — is stale, rank, foul, and were it not that those who woo her greet her with locked — closed — eyes, in spite of all the impostures, paintings, drugs, which her bawd Custom, aka Habit, daubs her cheeks with, she — personified Vice — would betray and reveal her loathed and leprous face, and frighten the enamored dotards away from themselves."

These dotards, aka imbeciles, were doting on themselves: They possessed Self-Love, although only one had so far drunk from the Fountain of Self-Love.

Criticus continued:

"But such is the perverseness of our nature, that if we once but fancy levity, how antique and ridiculous soever it may appear on us, yet will our muffled thought choose rather not to see its ridiculousness than to avoid it.

"And if we can just banish our own sense, we act our mimic — deceitful — tricks with that free license, that lust (that feeling of delight), that pleasure, that security as if we practiced in a pasteboard case, and no one saw the motion but the motion."

A motion is a puppet. The puppeteer is concealed in a pasteboard case and no one sees his motions as he manipulates the puppets. Because no one sees him, he can freely move as he likes.

A fool who does not know that he is a fool also acts freely. Because he is a fool, he does not see that his actions are foolish, and so he performs them.

Criticus continued:

"Well, check thy passion lest it grow too loud;

"While fools are pitied, they grow fat and proud."

CHAPTER 2

— 2.1 —

Cupid and Mercury spoke together.

"Why, this was most unexpectedly followed, my divine delicate Mercury," Cupid said. "By the beard of Jove, thou are a precious deity!"

Mercury said:

"Nay, Cupid, cease to speak improperly. Since we are turned cracks, let's study to be like cracks."

Cracks are cheeky children. Cupid and Mercury were disguised as pages: boy servants.

Cupid was speaking improperly because he was not speaking like a cheeky page. He needed to be cheekier and wittier and less complimentary. He also needed to talk to Mercury as if Mercury were a cheeky page and not a god.

Mercury continued:

"We must practice their language and behaviors, and not with a dead imitation. We must act freely, carelessly, and capriciously, as if our veins ran with quicksilver, and not utter a phrase but what shall come forth steeped in the very brine of conceit and sparkle like salt in fire."

"Quicksilver" is mercury, and mercurial people have sudden changes of mood. Think of the character Mercutio in Shakespeare's *Romeo and Juliet*.

Cupid replied, "Being cheeky and witty is not everyone's good fortune, Hermes. Though you can presume upon the easiness and dexterity of your wit, you shall give me permission to be a little solicitous of mine and allow me to not desperately hazard it after your capering humor."

"Nay then, Cupid, I think we must have you hoodwinked — blindfolded — again, for you are grown too provident and prudent since your eyes were at liberty," Mercury said.

"Not so, Mercury, I am still blind Cupid to thee," Cupid said.

"And what are you to the lady nymph you serve?" Mercury asked.

Cupid answered, "Indeed, I am 'page,' 'boy,' and 'sirrah.' These are all my titles."

"Then thou have not altered thy name with thy disguise?" Mercury asked.

"Oh, no, that would have been supererogation — too much," Cupid said. "You shall never hear your courtier called except by one of these three names."

"Indeed, then both our fortunes are the same," Mercury said.

"Why, what parcel — piece — of man have thou alighted on for a master?" Cupid asked.

"Such a one as, before I begin to decipher him, I dare not affirm him to be anything other than a courtier," Mercury said. "So much he is during this open time of revels that Cynthia has proclaimed, and he would be longer except that his means — his sources of income — are to leave him shortly afterward. His name is Hedon, and he is a gallant wholly consecrated to his pleasures."

"Hedon?" Cupid said. "He frequents my lady's chamber, I think."

"Tell me what she is called and then I can tell thee," Mercury said.

"She is Madam Philautia," Cupid said.

The name "Philautia" means "Self-Love."

Mercury said:

"Oh, aye, he affects her very particularly indeed.

"These are his graces: He does, besides me, keep a barber and a monkey."

Monkeys were fashionable pets.

Mercury continued:

He has a richly embroidered waistcoat to entertain his visitants in, with a cap almost suitable. His curtains and bedding are thought to be his own; his bathing tub is not suspected."

Hedon owned his own bath. Other courtiers might have a rented bath that had previously been used for treating some other people's venereal disease.

Mercury continued:

"He loves to have a fencer, a pedant, and a musician seen in his lodging in the mornings."

A pedant is a teacher.

"And not a poet?" Cupid asked.

Mercury answered:

"Fie, no! He himself is a rhymer, and that's a thought better than a poet."

He added:

"He is not lightly within to his mercer, no, although he comes when he takes medicine, which is commonly after his play."

A mercer sells silk and other fine fabrics. Hedon does not always come when his mercer calls, perhaps because the mercer is there to collect money he is owed.

The medicine is perhaps a purgative or an alcoholic drink.

The play could be in the theater or at a gambling table.

Mercury continued:

"He beats a tailor very well, but a stocking-seller admirably; and so, consequently, he beats anyone he owes money to who dares not resist him.

"He never makes general invitement — invitations — except in preparation for the publishing of — making known that he has — a new suit of clothing.

"By the Virgin Mary, then you shall have more drawn to his lodging than come to the launching of some three ships, especially if he is furnished with supplies for the retrieving of his old wardrobe from pawn; if he doesn't have the money that is needed to get his clothes out of the pawnshop, he rents a stock — suit — of apparel, and some forty or fifty pounds in gold for that afternoon to show."

A careless display of gold in one's home is a way to impress guests. Unfortunately for Hedon, he has to rent the gold.

Mercury continued:

"He's thought a very necessary perfume — accessory — for the presence chamber — the royal reception chamber — and only for that reason is he welcome thither: six milliners' shops won't give you the same scent."

Hedon smells good because of his perfume, and for that reason he is welcome in the royal reception room.

Mercury continued:

"He courts ladies with how many great horses he has ridden that morning, or how often he has done the whole or the half *pomado* in the seven-night — the week — before.

Hedon tries to impress ladies by telling them how many *pomados* he has performed. A *pomado* is a leap onto or over a horse's back; it is performed with the assistance provided by grabbing the saddle's pommel.

Mercury continued:

"And he sometimes ventures so far upon the virtue of his pomander — perfume ball — that he dares tell them how many shirts he has sweat through at tennis that week, but he wisely conceals so many dozen of balls he is on the score."

The score can be the result of the tennis game, but it can also be the tally of a debt. The balls may be the zeros in the figure owed.

Mercury continued:

"Here he comes, he who is all this."

Hedon, Anaides, and Gelaia entered the scene.

Hedon is a hedonistic courtier.

The name "Anaides" means "Shameless." He is an impudent courtier.

The name "Gelaia" means "Laughter." Laughter is the daughter of Folly. She was dressed in boys' clothing and served Hedon as a page.

"Boy!" Hedon called.

"Sir," Mercury answered.

Mercury was disguised as a young mortal, and he was serving Hedon as a page.

"Are any of the ladies in the presence chamber?" Hedon asked.

"None yet, sir," Mercury answered.

"Give me some gold," Hedon ordered.

Mercury gave him some gold.

Some servants carried the purses — the wallets — of their masters.

"Give me more gold," Hedon ordered.

Mercury gave him more gold, and then Mercury and Cupid stood to the side and watched the others.

"Is that thy serving-boy, Hedon?" Anaides asked.

"Aye, what do thou think of him?" Hedon answered.

"By God's heart, I'd geld him; I swear he has the philosopher's stone," Anaides said.

"Geld" means "castrate."

Alchemists sought the philosopher's stone, which was supposed to be able to turn base metals such as iron into precious metals such as gold.

In Ben Jonson's society, "stone" was slang for "testicle."

Mercury, being a god, although they did not know that, was able to supply Hedon with money — more money than Hedon actually had.

"Well said, my good melancholy devil," Hedon said to Anaides. "Sirrah, I have devised one or two of the prettiest oaths, this morning in my bed, as ever thou have heard, to use inside the presence chamber."

"Please, let's hear them," Anaides requested.

"Wait, thou shall use them before me," Hedon said.

"No," Anaides said. "If I do, then damn me. I have more oaths than I know how to utter, I swear by this air."

Hedon said, "Indeed, one is 'by the tip of your ear, sweet lady.' Isn't it pretty and genteel?"

"Yes, for the person it is applied to, a lady," Anaides said. "It should be light and —"

"Nay, the other is better, and it exceeds it by much," Hedon said. "The invention is farther fetched, too: 'By the white valley that lies between the Alpine hills of your bosom, I avow — etc.'"

Anaides said, "Well have you traveled — and travailed — for that phrase, Hedon."

In a translation of Ovid's *Banquet of Sense*, George Chapman used the phrase "Cupid's Alps" to describe the breasts of Corinna.

The travail may have been the trouble needed to steal the idea from Ovid.

Mercury said to himself, "Aye, he traveled in a map, where his eyes were but blind guides to his understanding, it seems."

Hedon said, "And then I have a salutation that will nick — outdo — all, by this dance-caper, ho!"

He leapt into the air.

"What salutation is that?" Anaides asked.

Hedon answered:

"You know I call Madam Philautia my 'Honor,' and she calls me her 'Ambition.'

"Now, when I meet her in the presence chamber, soon, I will come to her and say, 'Sweet Honor, I have hitherto contented my sense with the lilies of your hand, but now I will taste the roses of your lip,' and with that I will kiss her; to which she cannot but blushingly answer, 'Nay, now you are too ambitious.'

"And then I will reply, 'I cannot be too ambitious of honor, sweet lady.' Won't that be good? Huh? Huh?"

"Oh, assure your soul that it will," Anaides said.

"By heaven, I think it will be excellent, and a very politic achievement of a kiss," Hedon said.

"I have thought upon one for Moria of a sudden, too, if it take," Anaides said.

The name "Moria" means "Folly."

'What is it, my dear mischief?" Hedon said.

"By the Virgin Mary, I will come to her — and she always wears a muff if you remember — and I will tell her, 'Madam, your whole self cannot but be perfectly wise, for your hands have wit enough to keep themselves warm,'" Anaides said.

Hedon said:

"Now, before Jove, that is admirable! Look, thy page likes it, too, by Phoebus."

Anaides' page was Gelaia, who had laughed. Gelaia was dressed in a page's clothing.

Phoebus is Phoebus Apollo, who drives the chariot of the Sun.

Hedon continued:

"My sweet facetious rascal, I could eat water-gruel with thee for a month for this jest — oh, my dear rogue!"

Water-gruel is thin gruel made with water rather than milk.

Gruel made with milk is better.

Anaides said, "Oh, by Hercules, it is your only dish, above all your potatoes or oyster-pies in the world."

Hedon said:

"I have ruminated upon a most rare — splendid — wish, too, and the prophecy to it, but I'll have some friend to be the prophet, as thus: 'I wish that I were one of my mistress' *ciopinos*.'"

Ciopinos are shoes with a thick cork sole.

Hedon continued:

"Another demands, 'Why would he be one of his mistress' *ciopinos*?'

"A third answers, 'Because he would make her higher.'

"A fourth shall say, 'That will make her proud.'

"And a fifth shall conclude, 'Then do I prophesy, pride will have a fall, and he shall give it to her.'"

"Fall" was a double entendre with one meaning being falling backwards into the missionary position.

Hedon's wish was that Madam Philautia would go to bed with him.

Hedon wanted to set up a wish concerning Madam Philautia, but he needed help with it. A "prophet" would say the line about a wish that would set up Hedon's wish: "I wish that I were one of my mistress' *ciopinos*."

A prophet in this sense is like a straight man: The prophet prophesizes the punch line.

"I'll be your prophet," Anaides said. "By God's soul, it will be most exquisite! Thou are a fine inventious — inventive — rogue, sirrah."

"Nay, and I have posies for rings, too, and riddles that they dream not of," Hedon said.

Posies are short sayings that are engraved inside rings. For example: "As gold is sure, love is pure." "I love you." "*Amor vincit omnes*" [Love conquers all].

"Tut, they'll do that when they come to sleep on them — the riddles — for enough time," Anaides said. "But were thy devices never in the presence chamber yet, Hedon?"

"Oh, no, I disdain that," Hedon said.

Anaides said, "It would be good we went there ahead of time, then, and made them acquainted with the room where they shall act, lest the strangeness of it put them out of countenance when they should come forth."

The "devices" were the people who would assist Hedon in making his wish. They had not yet been in the presence chamber: the royal reception room.

Hedon, Anaides, and Gelaia exited.

Cupid asked, "Is that man a courtier, too?"

He was referring to Anaides.

Mercury said:

"In truth, no.

"He has two essential parts of the courtier: pride and ignorance. I mean of such a courtier who is indeed only the zany, aka clown, to an exact — perfect — courtier — by the Virgin Mary. His other parts come somewhat after the ordinary gallant."

The *Oxford English Dictionary* defines "zany" in this way:

"*A comic performer attending on a clown, acrobat, or mountebank, who imitates his master's acts in a ludicrously awkward way; a clown's or mountebank's assistant, a merry-andrew, jack-pudding; sometimes used vaguely for a professional jester or buffoon in general.*"

Mercury continued:

"Anaides is impudence itself. He is one who speaks all that comes in his cheeks and will blush no more than a sackbut. The words that come into his cheeks tend not to pass through his brain first."

A sackbut is 1) a wine barrel or 2) a musical instrument that is similar to a trombone.

Mercury continued:

"He lightly occupies the jester's room at the table and keeps laughter, Gelaia, a wench in page's attire, following him in place of a squire, whom he now and then tickles with some strange ridiculous stuff, uttered — as his land came to him — by chance.

"He will censure — judge to be good or bad — or discourse of anything, but as absurdly as you would wish.

"His fashion is not to take knowledge of a man who is beneath him in clothes. He pretends not to know him.

"He never drinks below the salt."

A salt cellar placed on a long table marked a division in status. Those seated above the salt had a higher social class than those seated below the salt. The host and hostess and their honored guests sat above the salt.

Mercury continued:

"He does naturally admire the wit of a man who wears gold lace or the rich cloth known as tissue, and he stabs any man who speaks more contemptibly of the scholar than he."

The play has no mention of Anaides ever stabbing any man who speaks more contemptibly of the scholar than he, and so it is likely that no man speaks more contemptibly of the scholar than he.

Mercury continued:

"He is a great proficient in all the illiberal sciences, such as cheating, drinking, swaggering, whoring, and such like.

"He never kneels except to pledge healths, nor prays except for a pipe of pudding-tobacco."

Pudding-tobacco was tobacco that had been pressed in rolls that resembled a sausage.

Mercury continued:

"He will blaspheme in his shirt even before he is fully dressed.

"The oaths that he vomits at just one supper would maintain a town with a garrison of profane soldiers in good swearing for a twelvemonth.

"One other genuine quality he has that crowns all these, and that is this: To a friend in need, he will not depart with the weight of a soldered groat, lest the world might judge him to be a prodigal or report that he is a gull — a fool."

A groat is a coin of little value. People would clip the edges of gold and silver coins to get some of the metal. Clipped coins could be repaired with solder.

Mercury continued:

"But by the Virgin Mary, he will give to his cockatrice or *punquetto*, half-a-dozen taffeta gowns or satin kirtles, aka skirts, in a pair or two of months — why, they are nothing."

A cockatrice and a *punquetto* are both prostitutes.

"I commend him," Cupid said. "He is one of my clients."

A person who would do such things is a follower of Cupid.

Amorphus, Asotus, and Cos entered the scene.

Amorphus said to Asotus, "Come, sir. You are now within sight of the presence chamber, and you see the privacy of this room, how sweetly it offers itself to our retired intendments — our private intentions."

He then said to Cos, "Page, cast a vigilant and inquiring eye about, so that we are not rudely surprised by the approach of some ruder stranger."

"I promise you, sir, that I'll tell you when the wolf enters," Cos said. "Fear nothing."

A Latin proverb stated, *lupus in fabula*: the wolf in the story. The wolf is a person who comes into a place suddenly while he or she is being gossiped about.

Mercury said quietly to Cupid, "Oh, what a mass of benefit shall we possess, in being the invisible spectators of this strange show now to be acted!"

They would be greatly entertained by witnessing what was about to happen.

Servants are sometimes treated as if they are invisible, but Mercury and Cupid are gods who have the power of making themselves invisible.

Amorphus said to Asotus:

"Plant yourself there, sir, and observe me.

"You shall now be the ocular-witness as well as the ear-witness [he would both see and hear] how clearly I can refel — refute — that paradox, or rather pseudodox, aka false teaching, of those who hold the face to be the index of the mind, which, I assure you, is not so in any politic — crafty — creature."

Some people believe that the face reveals the intentions of the person whose face it is, but Amorphus was going to show Asotus that he could put on and take off faces as he wished.

Amorphus continued:

"For instance, I will now give you the particular and distinct face of all of your most noted species of persons — as for example your merchant, your scholar, your soldier, your lawyer, courtier, etc. — and each of these so truly, as you would swear — except that your eye sees the variation of the lineament, aka facial features — that the expression were my most proper and genuine aspect.

"First, as for your merchant's, or city-face, it is thus."

He made a face like a merchant's face.

Amorphus continued:

"A merchant's face is a dull, plodding face, always looking in a direct line forward; there is no great matter in this face.

"Then you have your student's, or academic face, which is here."

He made a face like a student's face.

Amorphus continued:

"A student's face is an honest, simple, and methodical face, but somewhat more spread — broader — than the former.

"The third is your soldier's face."

He made a face like a soldier's face.

Amorphus continued:

"A soldier's face is a menacing and astounding face that looks broad and big; the grace of this face consists much in a beard.

"The anti-face — the opposite face — to this is your lawyer's face."

He made a face like a lawyer's face.

Amorphus continued:

"A lawyer's face is a contracted, subtle, and intricate face, full of quirks and turnings; a labyrinthian face, now angularly, now circularly, every way aspected.

"Next is your statist's — statesman's — face."

He made a face like a statesman's face.

Amorphus continued:

"A statesman's face is a serious, solemn, and supercilious face, full of formal and square gravity; the eye, for the most part, artificially and deeply shadowed; there is great judgment required in the making of this face.

"But now, to come to your face of faces, or courtier's face, it is of three sorts, according to our subdivision of a courtier: elementary, practic, and theoric.

"One kind is concerned with practice, and the other is concerned with theory.

"Your courtier theoric is he who has arrived to his farthest, and now knows the court rather by speculation — that is, contemplation — than practice, and this is his face: a fastidious, aka disdainful, and oblique face that looks as if it went with a vice and were screwed up like thus."

He made a face like a courtier theoric's face.

Amorphus continued:

"Your courtier practic is he who is yet in his path, his course, his way, and has not touched the punctilio or point of hopes; this face is here."

He made a face like a courtier practic's face.

Amorphus continued:

"A courtier practic's face is a most promising, open, smooth, and overflowing face, which seems as if it would run and pour itself into you.

"Your courtier elementary is one just newly entered or as it were in the alphabet, or ut-re-mi-fa-sol-la, of courtship; note well this face."

He made a face like a courtier elementary's face.

Amorphus continued:

"For it is this face — the courtier elementary's face — that you must practice."

"Ut-re-mi-fa-sol-la" is a musical scale; later, "doh" replaced "ut." One who practices the musical scale is likely a beginner.

"I'll practice them all, if you please, sir," Asotus said.

Amorphus said:

"Aye, hereafter you may, and it will not be altogether an ungrateful — unrewarding — study. For let your soul be assured of this: In any rank or profession whatsoever, the most general or major part of opinion goes with the face, and simply respects nothing else. Therefore, if that can be made exactly, curiously, exquisitely, thoroughly, it is enough.

"But, for the present, you shall apply yourself only to this face of the elementary courtier: a light, reveling, and protesting — one that frequently says, 'I protest,' aka 'I declare' — face, now blushing, now smiling, which you may help much with a wanton wagging of your head thus."

He wagged his head:

Amorphus continued:

"A feather will teach you how to wag your head.

"Or you may help that face much with kissing your finger that has the ruby, or playing with some string of your hatband, which is a most quaint kind of melancholy besides.

"Where is your page? Call for your casting-bottle — your perfume-bottle — and place your mirror in your hat, as I told you."

Asotus placed a small mirror in his hat.

Amorphus continued:

"Good.

"Come, don't look pale, observe me; set your face, and enter into the character of the elementary courtier."

Mercury said to himself, "Oh, for some excellent painter, to have painted the copy of all these faces!"

Asotus called for his page: "Prosaites!"

Amorphus admonished him: "Bah, I premonished — forewarned — you of that; in the court, say 'boy' or 'sirrah.'"

Prosaites entered the room.

Cos said to Amorphus, "Master, *lupus in* — Oh, it is Prosaites."

He had begun to say *"lupus in fabula"* to warn Amorphus about a newcomer, but then he saw that the newcomer was only Prosaites.

Asotus said to Prosaites:

"Sirrah, prepare my casting-bottle for me.

"I think I must be forced to purchase me another page; you see how Cos waits at hand here."

Cos was very close to Amorphus, while Prosaites had been so far from Asotus that Asotus had to call for him to come closer.

Amorphus, Asotus, Cos, and Prosaites exited.

"So will he, too, in time," Mercury said.

As time goes on, Asotus the prodigal will waste more and more of his wealth and grow closer and closer to Prosaites the beggar.

"Who's he, Mercury?" Cupid asked.

He was referring to Asotus.

Mercury answered:

"He is a notable finch, aka gullible fool. He is one who has newly entertained the beggar — Prosaites — to follow and serve him, but he cannot get him to wait near enough. He is Asotus, the heir of Philargyrus.

"But first I'll give you the other man's character, which may make his — Asotus' character — the clearer.

"The man who is with him is Amorphus, a traveler.

"He is a man so made out of the mixture and shreds of forms that he himself is truly deformed.

"He walks most commonly with a clove or toothpick in his mouth.

"He's the very mint of compliment; all his behaviors are printed, his face is another volume of essays, and his beard an Aristarchus."

Aristarchus was an ancient Greek critic who wrote commentaries.

Amorphus' face was a volume of essays, and his beard was the commentary on his face.

Just as clothing can reveal much information about social class, so can hair styles and beard styles. The Elizabethans sometimes starched their beards. But often beards were long and not starched. A person with a starched beard was concerned about fashion and so could be a courtier. Peasants would be unlikely to starch their beards.

A glance at Amorphus' beard would at least sometimes show whether the beard matched the face he was making.

Mercury continued:

"He speaks all cream, skimmed, and more affected than a dozen waiting women."

"All skimmed cream" means "all cream," and "all skimmed of cream" means "no cream."

Mercury continued:

"He's his own promoter in every place; the wife of the ordinary — an eating house — gives him his diet to maintain her table in discourse, which indeed is a mere tyranny over her other guests, for he will usurp all the talk — ten constables are not so tedious."

In Ben Jonson's society, constables had a reputation for dullness.

Mercury continued:

"He is no great shifter — changer — of clothing. Once a year his apparel is ready to revolt.

"He does act much to arbitrate quarrels, and he himself fights exceedingly well, out at a window."

The implication is that Amorphus does not fight so well when he is within arm's distance of the person he is willing to shout at from a window.

Mercury continued:

"He will lie cheaper than any beggar and louder than most clocks, for which he is right properly accommodated to the whetstone, his page."

Amorphus and his page, Cos, snore loudly.

Mercury then began to describe the character of Asotus:

"The other gallant — Asotus — is his zany, aka assistant to a clown, and does most of these tricks after him, sweats to imitate him in everything to a hair, except a beard, which is not yet extant."

Asotus is so young that he does not yet have a beard.

Mercury continued:

"Asotus learns to eat anchovies and caviar because Amorphus loves them.

"Asotus speaks as he — Amorphus — speaks.

"Asotus looks and walks, Asotus goes so in clothes and fashion, and Asotus is in all things, as if he — Asotus — were molded out of Amorphus.

"By the Virgin Mary, before they met, Asotus had other very pretty sufficiencies, aka competencies, which yet he retains some light impression of, as frequenting a dancing school and grievously torturing strangers with inquisition after his grace in his galliard — a French dance.

"Asotus buys a fresh acquaintance at any rate.

"His eye and his raiment confer much together as he goes in the street.

"He treads nicely, like a tightrope fellow who walks upon ropes, especially the first Sunday of his silk-stockings; and when he is most neat and new, you shall strip him of clothing with praise and commendations."

Amorphus had already stripped Asotus of his hat by praising it.

Cupid said, "Here comes another man."

Mercury said, "Aye, but he is a man of another strain, Cupid; this fellow weighs somewhat."

This new man is not a fool.

The new man was Criticus, who walked past Mercury and Cupid.

"What is his name, Hermes?" Cupid asked.

Mercury (Hermes) replied:

"His name is Criticus.

"Criticus is a creature of a most perfect and divine temper; he is one in whom the humors and elements are peaceably met without emulation of precedency.

"Criticus is neither too fantastically melancholy [sad], too slowly phlegmatic [unemotional and calm], too lightly sanguine [optimistic], nor too rashly choleric [angry], but in all things he is so composed and ordered that it is clear Nature was about some full work; she did more than make a man when she made him.

"His discourse is like his behavior, uncommon but not unpleasing; he is prodigal of neither discourse nor behavior.

"Criticus strives rather to be that which men call judicious than to be thought so; and he is so truly learned that he does not desire to show it off.

"Criticus will both think and speak his thought freely, but he is as distant from depraving — disparaging — any other man's merit as proclaiming his own.

"As for his valor, it is such that he dares as little to offer an injury as to receive one.

"In sum, he has a most ingenious — intelligent — and sweet spirit, a sharp and seasoned wit, a straight judgment, and a strong mind, constant and unshaken.

"Fortune could never break him or make him less.

"Criticus counts it his pleasure to despise pleasures, and he is more delighted with good deeds than goods. It is a competency — a sufficient reward — to him that he can be virtuous.

"Criticus neither covets nor fears; he has too much reason to do either — and that commends all things to him."

Cupid said, "Not better than Mercury commends him."

Mercury replied, "Oh, Cupid, it is beyond my deity to give him his due praises; I could leave my place in heaven to live among mortals, as long as I were sure to be no other than he is."

"By God's light, I believe he is your minion — your favorite," Cupid said. "You seem to be so ravished with him."

"He's one I would not willingly have a wry thought darted against," Mercury said.

Cupid said, "No, but a straight shaft in his bosom, I'll promise him, if I am Cytherea's son."

Cytherea is Venus. She was born in the surf near the island of Cythera, which is off the southwest coast of the Peloponnese in Greece. A temple on Cythera was dedicated to her.

"Shall we go, Cupid?" Mercury asked.

"Let's stay and see the ladies now; they'll come soon," Cupid said. "I'll help to paint them."

"Paint" can mean "makeup" as a noun and "put on makeup" as a verb, but Cupid was using the word to metaphorically mean "paint a verbal description of them."

"What, lay color upon color?" Mercury said. "That affords only an ill blazon."

Since one meaning of "color" is makeup, if Cupid were to literally paint the ladies' portrait, he would be using paint to paint their paint.

"Color" can also mean a heraldic device such as one painted on a metal blazon, aka war shield.

The word "blazon" can also mean "a portrait of a woman."

Argurion walked by them.

"Here comes metal to help it: the Lady Argurion," Cupid said.

"Argurion" means "silver," and since silver is used in the making of coins, it also means "money."

"Money, money," Mercury said.

Cupid said:

"The same.

"Argurion is a nymph of a most wandering and giddy disposition, as humorous as the air.

"She'll run from gallant to gallant, as they sit and play the card game primero in the presence chamber, most strangely, and she seldom stays with any.

"Argurion spreads money around as she goes.

"Today you shall have her look as clear and fresh as the morning, and tomorrow as melancholy as midnight.

"Argurion takes special pleasure in a close, obscure lodging, and for that reason visits the city so often, where she has many secret and true-concealing favorites."

Some people conceal the truth about her. Misers can pretend to be poor, and some spendthrifts can pretend to be wealthier than they are.

Cupid continued:

"When Argurion comes abroad, she's more loose and scattering — erratic — than dust, and she will fly from place to place as if she were rapt — seized — with a whirlwind.

"A young student, for the most part, she does not favor. She only greets him, and then leaves.

"A poet or a philosopher she is hardly brought to take any notice of, no, even though he may be some part of an alchemist."

No alchemist ever succeeded in making the philosopher's stone.

Cupid continued:

"Argurion loves a player well, and a lawyer infinitely, but your fool above all."

Players — gamblers — can get lucky at gambling sometimes.

Cupid continued:

"Argurion can do much in the court for the obtaining of any suit whatsoever; no door but flies open to her, her presence is above a charm.

"The worst in her is a lack of keeping state and maintaining dignity and too much descending into inferior and base offices. She's for any coarse employment you will put upon her, such as to be your procurer or pander or pimp."

Mercury said, "Quiet, Cupid, here comes more work for you, another character or two."

Cupid's work was introducing some new characters.

Phantaste, Moria, and Philautia entered the scene.

"Phantaste" means "Fantasy," which can mean Self-Delusion." She has a light wittiness.

"Moria" means "Folly." She is the mother of Gelaia, whose name means "Laughter." She is older than Phantaste and Philautia, who are of an age to be married soon.

"Philautia" means "Self-Love."

Phantaste said, "Wait, sweet Philautia, I'll just change my fan and go immediately."

She exited.

Moria said, "Now, in very good seriousness, ladies, I will have this order reversed; the presence chamber must be better maintained from you. A quarter past eleven and never a nymph in prospective — in view! Curse my hand, there must be a reformed discipline."

Moria perhaps wanted the nymphs — Phantaste and Philautia — to arrive before any other guests. They had arrived in the presence chamber only to find some men there first.

Moria then asked Philautia, "Is that your new ruff, sweet ladybird? By my truth, it is most intricately splendid."

Mercury and Cupid talked together at the side.

"Good Jove, what reverend gentlewoman in years might this be?" Mercury asked.

Cupid was the grandson of Jupiter, aka Jove.

Cupid said:

"This gentlewoman, Madam Moria, guardian of the nymphs, is one who is not now to be persuaded of her wit and intelligence."

Or lack of them.

In Queen Elizabeth I's court, the Mother of the Maids was responsible for taking care of the unmarried maidens of the court.

Cupid continued:

"She will think herself wise against all the judgments that come.

"She is a lady made all of voice and air, and she talks anything of anything.

"She is like one of your ignorant poetasters — inferior poets — of the time who, when they have got acquainted with a strange word, never rest until they have wrung it in, even though it loosens the whole fabric of their sense."

In other words, they pretensify the pretentiousness of their pretentoxicity.

Mercury said, "That was prettily and sharply noted, Cupid."

Cupid said:

"She will tell you that Philosophy was a fine reveler when she was young and he was a gallant, and that then, even though she is the one who says it, she was thought to be the Dame Dido and Helen of the court."

Dido, the Queen of Carthage, nearly kept the Trojan War survivor Aeneas from fulfilling his destiny of becoming an important founder of the Roman people.

Helen is Helen of Troy, whose beauty became a cause of the Trojan War when Paris ran off with her and took her to Troy. Her character was ambiguous: Some sources say she willingly left her legitimate husband, Menelaus, the King of Sparta, while other sources say she was kidnapped by Paris.

Cupid said:

"She will also speak about what a sweet dog she had this time four years ago, and how it was called Fortune, and that, if the Fates had not cut his thread, he would have been a dog to have given entertainment to any gallant in this kingdom."

The three Fates commanded the pulse of life; they controlled human life. Clotho spun the thread of life. Lachesis measured the thread of life, determining how long a person lived. Atropos cut the thread of life; when the thread was cut, the person died.

Ancient literature does not contain accounts of Atropos cutting the thread of life of a dog.

Moira's name is "Folly," and Fortune is a good name for Moira's dog. A proverb stated, "Fortune favors fools."

Mercury said, "Oh, please tell me no more about her. I am full of her."

Cupid said, "Yes, I must necessarily tell you that she composes a sack-posset well, and she would court a young page sweetly, except that her breath is against it."

Sack-posset is hot milk curdled with sack, a kind of white wine.

Moria had bad breath.

Mercury said:

"Now, may her breath, or something stronger, protect me from her!

"Tell me about the other, Cupid."

The other was Madam Philautia, Cupid's mistress, aka lady-boss. He served her as her page.

"Philautia" means "Self-Love."

Cupid said:

"Oh, that's my lady and mistress, Madam Philautia.

"She does not admire herself for any one particularity — particular thing — but for all:

"She is fair, and she knows that; she has a pretty light wit, too, and she knows that; she can dance, and she knows that, too; she can play at the game of shuttlecock, and she knows that, too.

"No quality she has but she shall take a very particular knowledge of and, most ladylike, commend it to you.

"You shall have her at any time read to you the history of herself, and she will very subtly run over another lady's sufficiencies — abilities — in order to come to her own.

"She has a good superficial judgment in painting, and she would like to appear to have such in poetry.

"She is a most complete lady in the opinion of some three people besides herself."

Philautia said to Moria, "Indeed, how did you like my quip to Hedon about the garter? Wasn't it witty?"

"Exceedingly witty and integrate," Moria replied. "You did so aggravate the jest with it — quite so."

Moria sometimes misused words. "Integrate" perhaps meant "complete." "Aggravate" perhaps meant "instigate."

"And didn't I dance movingly last night?" Philautia asked.

"Movingly!" Moria replied. "Out of measure, in truth, sweet lady."

Mercury said, "A happy commendation, to dance out of measure."

"Out of measure" can mean 1) outstandingly, or 2) out of time with the music. A measure is a type of stately dance.

Moria said, "Save only that you lacked the swim in the turn. Oh! When I was at fourteen —"

A "swim" is a smooth movement.

Philautia interrupted, "Nay, that's my own from any nymph in the court, I am sure of it, therefore you mistake me in that, guardian. Both the swim and the trip are properly mine. Everybody will affirm it who has any judgment in dancing, I assure you."

A trip is a dance movement.

Phantaste returned and said, "Come now, Philautia, I am ready. Shall we go?"

"Aye, good Phantaste," Philautia said. "What! Have you changed your headdress?"

"Yes, indeed; the other was so like the common style, it had no extraordinary grace," Phantaste replied. "Besides, I had worn it for almost a day, truly."

Philautia said, "I'll be sworn that it is most excellent for our project, and it is splendid. It is after the Italian print we looked at the other night."

The Italian print had shown an illustration of a headdress like the one Phantaste was wearing now.

"It is so," Phantaste said. "By this fan, I cannot abide anything that savors the poor overworn cut, anything that has any kindred with it. I must have variety, I must. I hate this mixing in fashion worse than to burn juniper in my chamber, I declare."

Juniper was burned as an aromatic. Juniper smoke was also thought to clean the air.

Philautia said, "And yet we cannot have a new peculiar court-attire, for if we attempt to do that, these retainers will imitate it — these suburb-Sunday-waiters, these courtiers for high days, aka festival days — I don't know what I should call them —"

Suburb-Sunday-waiters were people who visited the court on special days, but they were not in attendance daily, as were more important people.

Phantaste interrupted and said, "Oh, aye, they do most pitifully imitate; but I have a tire coming, indeed, that shall —"

Phantaste wore many headdresses. She changed her headdress because she had worn it almost a day, and she had a new headdress coming.

"Tire" can also mean "attire." Phantaste may have coming a new outfit of clothing that includes a new headdress.

Moria interrupted and said to Phantaste, "In good certain, madam, it makes you look most heavenly. But, lay your hand on your heart, you never skinned a new beauty more prosperously in your life, nor more supernaturally."

"Skinned a new beauty" perhaps meant putting on a new face of makeup.

Or "skinned a new beauty" perhaps meant putting on a new headdress or a new outfit of clothing. In that case, Phantaste would be the beauty in an outfit. Her beauty would be new because it was brought out by the new clothing.

Or Phantaste may have ordered an animal to be skinned so that its fur could be used in some clothing she was wearing.

Or Phantaste may have had a beauty rest to refresh her skin.

"Supernaturally" perhaps meant that Phantaste never looked more heavenly.

Moria said to Philautia, "Look, good lady, sweet lady, look."

She meant: Look at Phantaste.

Philautia said:

"It is very clear and well, believe me. But if you had seen mine yesterday when it was young, you would have —

"Who's your doctor, Phantaste?

This kind of doctor — an expert in an area of learning — may be a cosmetician.

Or this kind of doctor — an expert in an area of learning — may be a medical doctor.

Phantaste replied:

"Nay, that's counsel — that's a secret. Philautia, you shall pardon me.

"Yet I'll assure you that he's the most dainty, sweet, absolute, splendid man of the whole college. Oh! His very looks, his discourse, his behavior, all he does is medicine, I declare."

Philautia said, "For heaven's sake, what's his name? Good, dear Phantaste —"

Phantaste interrupted, "No, no, no, no, no, no! Believe me, not for a million of heavens. I will not make him cheap. Bah —"

Philautia, Phantaste, and Moria exited.

Cupid said about Phantaste, "There is a nymph, too, of a most curious and elaborate strain, light, all motion, an ubiquitary, she is everywhere, Phantaste —"

An ubiquitary is someone who is everywhere.

Mercury interrupted:

"Her very name speaks — describes — her; let her pass.

"But are these, Cupid, the stars of Cynthia's court? Do these nymphs — Philautia and Phantaste — attend upon Diana?"

Cupid replied:

"They are in her court, Mercury, but not as stars; these nymphs never come in the presence of Cynthia.

"The nymphs who make up Cynthia's train of attendants are the divine Arete [Excellence, Virtue], Timè [Honor], Phronesis [Prudence], Thauma [Wonder], and others of that high sort.

"These nymphs — Philautia and Phantaste — are privately brought in by Moria in this licentious time, against Cynthia's knowledge; and, like so many meteors, they will vanish when she appears."

This licentious time was the time of revels that Cynthia was permitting. It was a time of freedom.

Meteors are seen for only a short time. In Ben Jonson's society, comets were called meteors. The light of comets can be outshone and drowned out by the light of the Moon.

Prosaites, Gelaia, and Cos entered the scene. They were carrying bottles.

Prosaites sang:

"*Come follow me, my wags, and say as I say.*

"*There's no riches but in rags, hey day, hey day.*

"*You that [who] profess this art, come away, come away,*

"*And help to bear a part, hey day, hey day.*

"*Bear-wards [Bear-keepers] and blackingmen [sellers of shoe polish],*

"*Corn-cutters [cutters of corns on feet] and car-men [cart-men],*

"*Sellers of marking stones [chalk that was used to mark cattle so their owners could be identified],*

"*Gatherers-up of marrow bones [the marrow was edible],*

"*Pedlars [Peddlers] and puppet-players,*

"*Sow-gelders [Sow-spayers] and soothsayers,*

"*Gypsies and jailers,*

"*Rat-catchers and railers [scoffers],*

"*Beadles [minor parish officials] and ballad-singers,*

"*Fiddlers and fadingers [dancers of an Irish dance],*

"*Thomalins [itinerants] and tinkers,*

"*Scavengers and skinkers [bartenders],*

"*There goes the hare away,*

"*Hey day, hey day.*

"*Bawds and blind doctors,*

"*Paritors [ecclesiastical court officials] and spital proctors [hospital officials],*

"*Chemists [Alchemists] and cuttlebungs,*

"*Hookers and horn-thumbs —*"

These were types of thieves: Cuttlebungs used knives to cut the strings of purses (moneybags that could be tied to a person's belt), hookers used hooks to hook and steal items through open windows, and cuttlebungs used thimbles made of horn to protect their fingers as they cut purses.

Prosaites continued singing:

"*— with all cast [cast-off, jobless] commanders*

"*Turned post-knights [professional informers] or panders,*

"Jugglers and jesters,

"Borrowers of testers [six-pences],

"And all the troop of trash

"That're [Who're] allied to the lash [whipping was the trash's punishment],

"Come and join with your lags [fellows],

"Shake up your muscle-bags [thighs, or buttocks].

"For beggary bears the sway [is dominant],

"Then [So then] sing: cast care away,

"Hey day, hey day!"

Mercury said:

"What? Those who were our fellow pages just now are so soon promoted to be yeomen of the bottles?"

The yeomen of the bottles were literally the court officials who were in charge of the wine.

Mercury continued:

"The mystery, the mystery, good wags?"

The mystery was: What are you doing?

Cupid speculated, "Some diet — medicinal — drink they have the guard of."

Prosaites said, "No, sir, we are going in quest of a strange fountain lately found out."

"By whom?" Cupid asked.

"My master, or the great discoverer, Amorphus," Cos said.

"Thou have well entitled him a discoverer, Cos, for he will reveal all he knows," Mercury said.

The word "discover" can mean "reveal."

"Aye, and a little more, too, when the spirit is upon him," Gelaia said.

Yes, the alcoholic spirit. The "little more" than he knows will be lies.

Prosaites said, "Oh, the good travelling gentleman yonder — Amorphus — has caused such a drought in the presence chamber with reporting the wonders of this new water, that all the ladies and gallants lie languishing upon the rushes — floor covering — like so many impounded cattle in the midst of harvest to keep them from eating the crops, sighing one to another, and gasping, as if each of them expected a cock — a spout — from the fountain to be brought into his mouth; and, unless we return quickly, they are all, as a youth would say, no better than a few trouts cast ashore, or a dish of eels in a sandbag."

Mercury said:

"Well, then, you had best dispatch and have a care of them.

"Come, Cupid, thou and I will go peruse this dry wonder."

CHAPTER 3

— 3.1 —

Amorphus and Asotus entered the scene. Asotus had not made a good impression on the courtiers in or near the presence chamber. He had been tongue-tied.

Amorphus said to Asotus:

"Sir, don't let this discountenance or disgallant you — empty you of gallantry — a whit; you must not sink under the first disaster. It is with your young grammatical — as if still in grammar school — courtier as with your neophyte actor, a thing usual to be daunted at the first presence or inter-view."

An inter-view is also an enter-view. Asotus had entered and been inside this area that was frequently by courtiers for his first time, and the sight had daunted him.

Amorphus continued:

"There you saw Hedon and Anaides, who are far more practiced gallants than yourself, who were both out, aka at a loss of words, and that should comfort you.

"It is no disgrace to be discomfited, no more than for your adventurous reveler to fall by some inauspicious chance in his galliard, or for some subtle politician to undertake the bastinado, so that the state might think worthily of him and respect him as a man well beaten to the world."

A galliard is a dance in triple time.

The bastinado was a Turkish punishment in which a person was beaten on the feet.

A man who is well beaten to the world may be a man who is well traveled and has beaten a path to various parts of the world. One would have to travel to undergo the bastinado.

Amorphus continued:

"What, has your tailor provided the property — the outfit — we spoke of at your chamber, or not?"

"I think he has," Asotus said.

Amorphus said:

"Nay, I entreat you, don't be so flat and melancholic. Erect your mind. Rouse yourself. You shall redeem this with the courtship I will teach you in preparation for this afternoon.

"Where will you eat today?"

"Wherever you please, sir, anywhere, I say," Asotus said.

Amorphus said:

"Come, let us go and taste some light dinner, a dish of sliced caviar or so."

Normally, caviar is eaten as a garnish or a spread. It can be eaten with sliced foods such as bread or salmon.

Amorphus continued:

"And after we eat, you shall practice an hour at your lodging some few forms that I have remembered. If you had but so far gathered your spirits to you as to have taken up a rush from the floor, when you were out, and wagged it like this —"

He demonstrated by picking up a rush — a plant whose stalks were used as floor coverings — from the floor and wagging it.

Amorphus continued:

"— or cleaned your teeth with it, or just turned aside and feigned some business to whisper with your page until you had recovered yourself, or just had found some slight stain in your stocking or any other pretty invention, so long as it had been sudden, you might have come off with a most clear and courtly grace."

Asotus said, "A poison of all, I think, I was forspoke — I was bewitched! I was!"

"Forspeak" means "speak evil of" as well as "bewitched."

Amorphus said:

"No, I do partly aim at the cause, which was ominous indeed: For as you enter at the door, there was opposed to you the form of a wolf in the wall hangings, which, your eye taking suddenly, gave a false alarm to the heart, and that was what called your blood out of your face and so disordered the whole rank of your spirits.

"I urge you to labor to forget it."

They exited.

Hedon and Anaides talked together. Hedon had conceived a deep dislike of Criticus. Hedon was a hedonistic courtier, and Anaides was an impudent courtier.

They had been in the same place as Amorphus and Asotus, and Hedon had also been discomfited. Hedon and Anaides had planned a way for Hedon to compliment his mistress — the woman he admired — Madam Philautia. The plan, however, had not gone well.

Hedon said, "By God's heart, was there ever so prosperous an invention — my plan — thus unluckily perverted and spoiled by a whoreson bookworm, a candle-waster?"

He was talking about Criticus, although he did not know his name.

Some people "waste" candles by using their light to study at night.

Anaides replied, "Nay, don't be impatient, Hedon."

"By God's light, I would like to know his name," Hedon said.

Anaides said:

"Hang him, the poor grogram-wearing rascal. Please don't think about him."

Grogram is a coarse cloth of the type that a scholar could wear.

Anaides continued:

"I'll send for him to come to my lodging, and have him blanketed whenever thou wish, man."

Some disliked men were put in a blanket and tossed high in the air.

"By God's soul, I wish thou could," Hedon said. "Look, here he comes. Laugh at him, laugh at him. Ha, ha, ha!"

Criticus passed by them and stood to the side.

Anaides said, "Bah, he smells like lamp-oil because of his studying by candlelight."

"How confidently he went by us, and how carelessly!" Hedon said. "He was never moved, nor stirred to anger at anything! Did you observe him?"

"Aye, a pox on him," Anaides said. "Let him go, dormouse; he is in a dream now. He has no other time to sleep but thus when he walks abroad to take the air."

Dormice were known for sleeping much of the time.

Anaides may have meant to say, "Let him go — the dormouse." If he had, then the "dormouse" would be Criticus, not Hedon.

Hedon said, "By God's precious blood, this afflicts me more than all the rest, that we should so particularly direct our hate and contempt against him, and he to carry it thus without wound or passion! It is insufferable."

Criticus was unconcerned about what they thought of him.

Anaides said, "By God's eyelid, my dear Envy, if thou will just say the word now, I'll undo and ruin him eternally for thee."

"How, sweet Anaides?" Hedon asked.

"By the Virgin Mary, half a score of us will get him in one night and make him pawn his wit for a supper," Anaides answered.

They would get Criticus to speak entertainingly while being fed a meal. Apparently, Anaides thought that Criticus would make a fool of himself. Or, possibly, they thought that Criticus would flatter anyone who bought him a meal.

Hedon said:

"Get out! Go away! Thou have such unseasonable jests!

"By this heaven, I wonder at nothing more than our gentlemen ushers, who will allow a piece of serge or perpetuana to come into the presence chamber. I think that they should, out of their experience, better distinguish the silken disposition of a courtier than to let such terrible coarse rags mix with them, able to fret — fray — any smooth or genteel society to the threads with their rubbing devices — their irritating conversation."

Serge and perpetuana are rough kinds of cloth that a scholar might wear.

Anaides said, "Damn me if I should adventure — come — on his company once more without a suit of buff — thick leather — to defend my wit. He does nothing but stab, the slave. How mischievously he crossed thy device of the prophecy there! And Moria came without her muff, too, and there my invention was lost."

"Well, I have decided what I'll do," Hedon said.

"What, my good spirituous spark — my spirited gallant?" Anaides asked

"By the Virgin Mary, I'll speak all the venom I can of him, and poison his reputation in every place where I come," Hedon said.

He would maliciously gossip about him.

"Before God, that is most courtly," Anaides said.

Courtly behavior is supposed to be behavior that shows good etiquette, but some courtiers at this court engaged in malicious gossip.

Hedon added, "And if I chance to be present where any question is made of his sufficiencies and abilities, or of anything he has done in private or public, I'll censure — judge — it slightly, and ridiculously —"

Anaides replied:

"At any hand, beware of that, lest you may draw your own judgment into suspicion."

The judgment of Criticus was much better than the judgment of Hedon.

Anaides continued:

"No, I'll instruct thee in what thou shall do, and by a safer, more secure means: Approve anything thou hear of his according to the received opinion of it. If other people think it is good, then you also say that it is good.

"But if what he says is extraordinarily good, give the credit of it not to him but to some other person whom thou more particularly like.

"That's the way to plague him, and he shall never come to defend himself.

"By God's blood, I'll give out the gossip that all he says is dictated from — that is, he copied the conversation of — other men; and I'll swear it, too, if thou shall allow me to, and I'll swear that I know the time and place where he stole it.

"Although my soul is not guilty of believing any such thing, and although I think, from the bottom of my heart, he hates such barren shifts and imaginative tricks as plagiarism; yet to do thee a pleasure and him a disgrace, I'll damn myself, or do anything."

Hedon said, "Many thanks, my dear devil. We'll put it seriously in practice, indeed."

Criticus had overheard their conversation.

Alone, he said to himself:

"Do, good Detraction — Anaides — do, and I the while

"Shall shake thy spite off with a careless — worry-free — smile.

"Poor piteous — contemptible — gallants, what lean idle sleights and tricks their thoughts suggest to flatter their starved hopes!

"As if I didn't know how to entertain these straw-devices — harmless plots — but of force must yield to the weak stroke of their calumnious and abusive tongues.

"Why should I care what every dor — fool — buzzes of gossip into credulous ears?

"It is a crown — a mark of distinction — to me that the best judgments can report me wronged, them liars, and their slanders impudent.

"Perhaps, upon the rumor of their speeches, some grieved friend will whisper, 'Criticus, men speak ill of thee.'

"As long as they are ill men, if they spoke worse of me, it would be better, for to be dispraised and criticized by such men is the most perfect praise.

"What can his censure hurt me — the censure of a man whom the world has censured vile before me?

"Censured" means "judged."

Criticus continued:

"If good Chrestus [Honest], Euthus [Straightforward], or Phronimus [Sensible] had spoken the words, they would have moved me, and I should have called my thoughts and actions to a strict account upon the hearing.

"But when I remember it is Hedon and Anaides, alas, then, I think but who and what they are, and I am not stirred to anger:

"The one is a light voluptuous reveler.

"The other is a strange arrogating puff of nothing.

"Both are impudent and ignorant enough.

"They are courtiers who talk as they are accustomed to talk, not as I merit and deserve.

"They instead traduce by habit just as most dogs bark by custom.

"They do nothing out of judgment, but out of disease.

"They speak ill because they never could speak well.

"And who would be angry with this race of creatures? What wise physician have we ever seen moved by a frantic man? The same feelings that a wise physician bears to his sick patient a right mind should carry to such as these.

"And I count it a most rare revenge that I can thus, with such a sweet neglect, pluck from them all the pleasure of their malice.

"For that's the mark — the target — of all their enginous craft — their deceitful plots — to wound my patience, howsoever they seem to aim at other objects, which if missed, their envy's like an arrow shot upright, an arrow which in the fall endangers their own heads."

Arete entered the scene.

The name "Arete" means "Excellence" or "Virtue." Lady Arete is wise.

"What, Criticus!" Arete said. "Where have you spent the day? You have not visited your jealous friends!"

In Ben Jonson's society, one meaning of "jealous" is "anxious for your welfare."

Criticus replied:

"I have been where I have seen, most honored Arete, the strangest pageant, fashioned like a court — at least I dreamt I saw it — so diffused and disordered, so painted with makeup, so outfitted in fools' pied — multi-colored — clothing, and so full of rainbow strains and streaks of color, as never yet, either by time or place, was made the food to my distasted — disgusted — sense.

"Nor can my weak, imperfect memory now render to my tongue half the forms that were convolved — coiled together — within this thrifty — fertile — room."

The room was fertile ground for a satirist such as Ben Jonson.

Criticus then began to list a few types of people whom he had seen by the presence chamber:

"Here stalks by me a proud and spangled-clothing sir who looks three hands-breadths higher than the top of his head. He savors himself alone, is only kind and loving to himself. He is one who will speak darker and more doubtful — ambiguous — than six oracles. He salutes a friend as if he had a stitch of sudden pain. He is his own chronicle, and he scarcely can eat because he is busy registering himself."

This courtier who is his own chronicle and is constantly registering himself is someone who constantly writes notes, perhaps to remember things to write in a journal later.

The parish would register — keep a record of — important events, including births, weddings, and deaths.

Criticus continued:

"He is waited on by mimics [buffoons], jesters, panders, parasites and hangers-on, and other such-like prodigies — monsters — of men.

"This courtier having gone past, there comes some subtle Proteus."

Proteus is a mythological sea-god who is a shape-shifter: He can change his shape into many other forms.

Criticus continued:

"He is one who can change and vary with all the forms he sees. He can be anything but honest, serves the time by following whatever is the current fashion, hovers between two factions, and explores the plots of both. With cross — opposite — faces, he bears news of these plots to the divided heads, and he is received with mutual grace by either head."

This type of courtier plays both sides. When two factions are opposed, he will present one face to the head of one faction and an opposite face to the head of the other faction. In each case, he seems to favor the faction of the person to whom he is speaking and not favor the other faction.

Criticus continued:

"He is one who dares do deeds worthy the hurdle or the wheel, to be thought somebody; and is, in truth, such as the satirist points truly forth:

"'*Criminibus debent hortos, praetoria, mensas.*'"

The hurdle was a sled on which a convicted criminal was drawn to the place of execution.

To be broken on the wheel was to be bound to a wheel and endure the breaking of one's bones. Or a person could be tied up and an executioner would drop a heavy wheel on the person and break that person's bones.

The Latin quotation, which is from Juvenile, Satire 1, line 75, means "To their crimes they owe their gardens, their palaces, and their tables."

"You tell us wonders, Criticus," Arete said.

Criticus replied:

"Tut, this is nothing.

"There stands a neophyte, glazing of his face — that is, making his face sleek — in preparation for when his idol — the woman he loves — enters, and repeats, like an unperfect prologue at third music, his part of speeches and confederate jests in passion — passionately — to himself."

"An unperfect prologue at third music" is a prologue speaker who is imperfect — that is, he hasn't memorized his lines properly. "Third music" was the signal for the speaker to begin saying his prologue at the beginning of a play.

"Confederate jests" are those that need a collaborator to set up the jest or witticism. An example of a confederate jest is the one about *ciopinos* in which Hedon needed the assistance of Anaides.

Criticus continued:

"Another swears his scene of courtship over, and then seems as if he would kiss away his hand in kindness."

Courtiers would sometimes kiss their own hand.

Criticus continued:

"A third is most in action, swims and frisks, plays with his mistress' paps, aka breasts, salutes her pumps, aka shoes, and will spend his patrimony — inheritance — for a garter, or the least feather in her bounteous fan.

"A fourth, he comes in only to act as a mute, divides the act with a dumb show, and exits."

The acts of some Elizabethan plays were divided by a dumb show in which the actors did not speak. A mute is a character that does not speak.

Criticus continued:

"Then must the ladies laugh, but straightaway comes their scene, a six-times-worse confusion than the rest.

"Where you shall hear one woman talk about this man's eye, another woman talk about his lip, a third woman talk about his nose, a fourth commend his leg, a fifth his foot, a sixth his hand, and everyone commends a limb, so that you would think the poor distorted gallant must there expire.

"Then they fall in discourse about tires — headdresses — and fashions: how and in which order of social prominence they must take their places, where they may kiss [!], and whom; when to sit down, and with what grace to rise; and if they greet someone, what courtesy they must use.

"They talk such cobweb stuff as would force the commonest sense to abhor the Arachnean workers."

Arachne was a Greek woman who out of pride challenged the goddess Athena to a weaving contest. Arachne created a weaving with no flaws, and Athena turned her into a spider that created light, airy cobwebs.

The court ladies — the Arachnean workers — described by Criticus are proud and without substance.

Arete said:

"Have patience, Criticus.

"This knot of spiders will be soon dissolved, and all their webs swept out of Cynthia's court when once her glorious deity appears and just presents herself in her full light.

"Until then, go in, and spend your hours with us your honored friends, Timè [Honor] and Phronesis [Prudence], in contemplation of our goddess' name."

The goddess' name is Cynthia, and Arete, Timè, and Phronesis honored her and her name.

Arete then asked Criticus to create an entertainment to honor Cynthia.

Arete continued:

"Think on some sweet and choice artistic invention now that is worthy her serious and lustrous and illustrious eyes, so that from the merit of it we may take the desired occasion to prefer and promote your worth, and make your service known to Cynthia.

"It is the pride of Arete to grace her studious lovers, and in scorn of time, envy, and ignorance, to lift her studious lovers' state and condition above a vulgar height.

"True happiness consists not in the multitude of friends, but in their worth and choice; nor would I have Virtue pursue a popular regard.

"Let them be good who love me, although they may be but few."

Criticus said, "I kiss thy hands, divinest Arete, and vow myself to thee and Cynthia."

Amorphus and Asotus talked together. A tailor was present who had brought Asotus the clothing he had ordered.

Amorphus said to Asotus, "A little more forward, so, sir."

He meant, Look more confident.

He then said to Asotus, 'Now, go in, take off your cloak yourself, and come forth."

Asotus exited.

Amorphus then said, "Tailor, bestow thy absence upon us, and be not prodigal of this secret except to a dear customer."

Amorphus did not want news of Asotus' new suit of clothing to get out before Asotus had made a grand appearance in the presence chamber.

The tailor exited, and Asotus returned.

Amorphus began to teach Asotus about courtly behavior and about wooing a court lady:

"It is well entered, sir — you are making a good entrance.

"Stay, you come on too fast; your pace is too impetuous.

"Imagine this to be the palace of your pleasure, or place where your lady is pleased to be seen. First, you present yourself, thus —"

He demonstrated.

Amorphus continued:

"— and, spying her, you fall off, aka withdraw, and walk some two turns around the area; in which time it is to be supposed your passion has sufficiently whited your face.

"Then, stifling a sigh or two and closing your lips, with a trembling boldness and bold terror, you advance yourself forward.

"Try thus much, I ask you to."

Affected by his love for his lady, whoever she may be, when Asotus saw her, he was supposed to turn pale and tremble.

Asotus said, "Yes, sir, I pray to God that I can light on it and get it right. Here I come in, you say, and present myself?"

"Good," Amorphus said.

"And then I spy her and walk off?" Asotus asked.

"Very good," Amorphus said.

"Now, sir, I stifle a sigh and advance forward?" Asotus asked.

"Trembling," Amorphus said.

Asotus replied, "Yes, sir, trembling. I shall do it better when I come to it. And what must I speak now?"

Amorphus answered, "By the Virgin Mary, you shall say, '*Dear beauty*,' or '*Sweet honor*,' or by what other title you please to remember her, 'I think you are melancholy.' This is what you will say if she is alone now and discompanied — without any company."

"Well, sir, I'll enter again," Asotus said. "Her title shall be 'My dear Lindabrides.'"

"Lindabrides?" Amorphus asked.

Lindabrides was a character in a romance that Margaret Tyler translated as *The Mirrour of Knighthood*. Lindabrides was the Princess of Tartary.

Asotus explained, "Aye, sir, the Emperor Alicandro's daughter, and the Prince Meridian's sister, in *The Knight of the Sun*. She should have been married to him, except that the Princess Claridiana —"

Lindabrides is a kinda, but not quite a, bride. Asotus remembered that she was unlucky in love. In the romance, she spends a lot of time weeping.

"Lindabrides" is also known as a name for a mistress, in the sense of "lady-love."

"Oh, you betray your reading," Amorphus said.

One meaning of "betray" is "reveal." Another is "be false to."

Asotus said:

"Nay, sir, I have read history, I am a little humanitian."

By "humanitian," he meant "student of the humanities."

Asotus continued:

"Don't interrupt me, good sir."

He then said what he would say to his loved one:

"*My dear Lindabrides — my dear Lindabrides — my dear Lindabrides, I think you are melancholy*."

Amorphus said, "Aye, and take her by the rosy-fingered hand."

Homer's *Odyssey* refers to "rosy-fingered dawn."

Asotus said:

"Must I do so?

"Oh, '*My dear Lindabrides, I think you are melancholy.*'"

Amorphus said:

"Or say this, sir:

"'*May all variety of divine pleasures, choice sports, sweet music, rich fare, brave attires [outfits], soft beds, and silken thoughts attend this dear beauty.*'"

Asotus said:

"Believe me, that's pretty!

"'*May all variety of divine pleasures, choice sports, sweet music, rich fare, brave attires [outfits], soft beds, and silken thoughts attend this dear beauty.*'"

Amorphus continued to offer wooing advice, using some military metaphors:

"And then, offering to kiss her hand, if she shall coyly **recoil**, and signify your **repulse**, you are to **re-enforce** yourself with these words:

"'*More than most fair lady, let not the rigor of your just disdain thus coarsely censure of your servant's zeal*'; and, in addition, profess her to be '*the only and absolute unparalleled creature I*' — that is, you — '*do adore, and admire, and respect, and reverence in this court, corner of the world, or kingdom.*'"

"This is hard, by my faith," Asotus said. "I'll begin it all again."

"Do so, and I will act the part of your lady," Amorphus said.

Pleased, Asotus said:

"Will you grant me the favor of playing the lady, sir?"

In the character of the wooer, Asotus said:

"'*May all variety of divine pleasures, choice sports, sweet music, rich fare, brave attire, soft beds, and silken thoughts attend this dear beauty.*'"

In the character of the lady, Amorphus said:

"'*So, sir, please go away.*'"

In the character of the wooer, Asotus said:

"'*More than most fair lady, let not the rigor of your just disdain thus coarsely censure of your servant's zeal. I say that you are the only and absolute unapparelled*' —"

"Unapparelled' " means "naked."

Amorphus corrected him, "Unparalleled."

In the character of the wooer, Asotus said:

"'*Unparalleled creature, I do adore, and admire, and respect, and reverence in this court, corner of the world, or kingdom.*'"

Amorphus said:

"This is, if she abides — is waiting for — you.

"But now, let's assume that she should be *passant* [passing by] when you enter, as thus" — he demonstrated — "then you are to frame your gait thereafter, and call upon her, '*Lady, nymph, sweet refuge, star of our court.*'

"Then if she be *guardant* [on guard]" — he demonstrated — "you are to come on and, laterally disposing yourself, swear '*by her blushing and well-colored cheek, the bright dye of her hair, her ivory teeth,*' or some such white and innocent oath to induce you.

"If she is *reguardant* [on guard and facing you]" — he demonstrated — "then maintain your station, brisk and irpe [typo for 'ripe,' aka mature], show the supple motion of your pliant body, but, in chief, of your knee and hand, which cannot but arride — gratify — her proud humor exceedingly."

The situation may be that the lady is carefully looking at Asotus to see if he would be a good sex partner. He would show off his supple body, including the parts — knees and hands — that he would use to hold himself up in the missionary position. He would be making the case that he could gratify her by riding her and making her feel gratified and proud because she is wanted sexually.

Asotus said, "I conceive you, sir. I shall perform all these things in good time, I don't doubt, they do so hit — impress — me."

Amorphus said:

"Well, sir, I am your lady.

"Make use of any of these beginnings, or some other out of your own invention, and prove how you can hold up and follow it.

"Say, say."

Asotus knelt and said, "Yes, sir."

In the character of the wooer, Asotus began:

"'*My dear Lindabrides*' —"

Amorphus interrupted:

"No, you affect that Lindabrides too much, and, let me tell you, it is not so courtly. Your pedant — scholar — should provide you some parcels of French, or some pretty commodity of Italian to commence with, if you want to be exotic and exquisite."

Asotus said, "Yes, sir, he was at my lodging the other morning; I gave him a doublet — a jacket."

Amorphus responded:

"Double your benevolence, and give him the hose — the leggings — too. If you clothe his body, he will help to apparel your mind.

"But now, see what your proper genius — your own guiding spirit — can perform alone, without adjection — without the addition — of any other Minerva."

"I understand, sir," Asotus said.

Amorphus said, "I do stand — support — you, sir; fall back to your first place."

Asotus stood up and assumed the first posture he had been taught.

Amorphus said, "Good, surpassingly well, very properly pursued."

In the character of the wooer, Asotus said:

"*Beautiful, ambiguous, and sufficient lady. What, are you all alone?*"

"Ambiguous" and "sufficient" are poor words to use to compliment a lady.

In the character of the lady, Amorphus said:

"*We would be, sir, if you would leave us.*"

In the character of the wooer, Asotus began:

"*I am at your beauty's appointment, bright angel; but —*"

In the character of the lady, Amorphus interrupted:

"*But what?*"

In the character of the wooer, Asotus said:

"*No harm, more than most fair feature.*"

"That touch relished well," Amorphus said.

A "touch" is a hit in fencing.

In the character of the wooer, Asotus began:

"*But, I protest* —"

In the character of the lady, Amorphus interrupted:

"*And why should you protest?*"

In the character of the wooer, Asotus said:

"*For good will, dear esteemed madam, and I hope Your Ladyship will so conceive of it — if ever you have seen great Tamburlaine.*"

Tamburlaine was a violent man in Christopher Marlowe's plays *Tamburlaine, Part One* and *Tamburlaine, Part Two*. If Tamburlaine wants a lady to conceive of something, or to conceive, the lady would be well advised to do it — out of fear.

Amorphus said:

"Oh, that line of blank verse was excellent! If you could pick out more of these play-particles, aka pieces of plays, and, as occasion shall greet you, embroider or damask — ornament — your discourse with them, persuade your soul, it would judiciously commend you.

"Come, this was a well-discharged and auspicious bout. Prove the second. Let have a second bout."

In the character of the wooer, Asotus said:

"*'Lady, I cannot swagger it in black and yellow.'*"

Malvolio wears black clothes and yellow stockings in Shakespeare's *Twelfth Night*. He thinks the yellow stockings are what the woman he wants to marry wants him to wear. They aren't.

In the character of the lady, Amorphus said:

"*'Why, if you can revel it in white, sir, it is sufficient.'*"

In the character of the wooer, Asotus said:

"*'Say you so, sweet lady? Lan, tede de, de, dant, dant, dant, dante, etc. No, in good faith, madam, whosoever told your ladyship so, abused you; but I would be glad to meet your ladyship in a measure.'*"

A measure is a stately dance.

The English word "lante" means "bestows." The Italian word *tediante* means "wearisome" and "boring." Many ladies would likely think that Asotus' wooing bestows wearisomeness and boredom.

In the character of the lady, Amorphus said:

"*'Me, sir? Perhaps you measure me by yourself, then?'*"

In the character of the wooer, Asotus said:

"*'I wish I might, fair feature.'*"

In the character of the lady, Amorphus said:

"*'And what were you the better, if you might?'*"

In the character of the wooer, Asotus said:

"*'The better it please you to ask, fair lady.'*"

Amorphus said:

"Why, this was ravishing, and most acutely continued.

"Well, don't spend your humor too much; you have now competently exercised your conceit.

"This kind of exercise, once or twice a day, will render you an accomplished, elaborate, and well-levelled — poised — gentleman.

"Convey in your courting-stock — take me to the ladies; we will, in the heat of this, go visit the nymphs' chamber."

CHAPTER 4

— 4.1 —

Phantaste, Philautia, Argurion, Moria, and Cupid, who was still disguised as a page, were in a room together. The ladies were seated on chairs and couches. They were waiting for the water from the fountain to be brought to them.

"I wish this water would at once arrive that our travelling friend so commended to us," Phantaste said.

"So would I, for he has left all of us in travail with expectation of it," Argurion said.

"I pray to Jove that I will never rise from this couch if ever I thirsted more for a thing in my whole time of being a courtier," Phantaste said.

A courtier is an attendant at court. Women can be courtiers. They can be ladies of the court.

Philautia said, "Nor will I, I'll be sworn; the very mention of the water sets my lips in a worse heat than if he had sprinkled them with mercury."

The chemical element mercury was used as a cosmetic. It could blister and cause a rash.

She then ordered her page, "Reach me the glass, sirrah."

Cupid handed her a glass and said, "Here, lady."

Moria asked, "Philautia, your lips don't peel, sweet charge, do they?"

"Yes, they peel a little, guardian," Philautia answered.

"Oh, it is an imminent good sign," Moria said. "Whenever my lips peel, I am sure to have some delicious good drink or other approaching."

Argurion said, "By the Virgin Mary, this sign may be a good sign for us ladies; for, it seems, the fountain water is far-fetched and fetched from afar by their delay in returning."

"I bet my palate against yours, dear Honor, that the water shall prove to be most elegant, I assure you," Moria said. "Oh, I do fancy this gear — this thing, the water — that's long in coming, with an unmeasurable strain."

Phantaste said:

"Please sit thee down, Philautia.

"That rebato — your stiff collar — becomes thee singularly."

"Isn't it quaint?" Philautia said.

"Yes, indeed," Phantaste said.

She added, "I think thy servant Hedon is not at all as obsequious to thee as he used to be. I don't know why, but he's grown out of his garb — his clothing — lately. He's warped."

A "servant" in this context is a man who loves a woman and serves her.

"Warp" and "weft" are terms used in weaving.

Moria said, "In trueness, I think so, too. He's much converted and changed."

Philautia replied:

"Tut, let him be what he will; he is an animal I dream not of.

"This tire — headdress — I think, makes me look very ingenuously — that is, ingeniously — quick, and spirited; as if I should be some Laura or some Delia, I think."

The Italian poet Petrarch loved Laura. He wrote about her in *Rerum vulgarium fragmenta* (*Fragments of Vernacular Matters*).

The poet Samuel Daniel wrote a sonnet sequence about Delia titled "To Delia."

Moria said, "As I am wise, the fair honors that Philautia gave Hedon to be her Ambition spoiled him. Before, he was the most propitious and observant young novice —"

Phantaste interrupted:

"— no, no; you are the whole heaven awry, guardian. It is the swaggering tilt-horse — that Anaides — who draws with him there who has been the diverter of him."

Phantaste thought that Anaides had corrupted Hedon, who then diverted his attention away from Philautia.

In Phantaste's image, Hedon and Anaides are yoked together.

Tilt-horses are used in jousting tournaments.

Philautia said, "For Cupid's sake, speak no more about him. I wish I might never dare to look in a mirror again if I ever respect a marmoset — small monkey — of them all, otherwise than I would respect a feather or my shuttlecock, to make fun and entertainment of now and then."

Phantaste said:

"Come sit down.

"Indeed, if you are good beauties, let's run over and discuss all of them — all the men — now.

"Which man is the properest — most handsome — man among them? I say the traveler, Amorphus."

They looked at pictures of the male courtiers.

Philautia said, "Oh, fie on him. He looks like a Dutch trumpeter in the sea battle of Lepanto in the gallery yonder, and he speaks to the tune of a country lady who comes always in the rearward or train of a fashion."

"I should have judgment in a feature, sweet beauties," Moria said.

"A body would think so, at these years of yours," Phantaste said.

Moria was older than the other women present.

"And I prefer another now, far before him, a million at least," Moria said.

"Who might that be, guardian?" Phantaste asked.

"By the Virgin Mary, fair charge, I prefer Anaides," Moria answered.

Phantaste said:

"Anaides? You talked of a tune, Philautia.

"Anaides is one who speaks in a key, like the opening of some justice's gate or a post-boy's horn, as if his voice feared an arrest for some ill words it should give and were loath to come forth."

The gate of a justice may creak when it opens or when a key turns in its lock.

A post-boy's horn is loud.

Anaides the impudent courtier may be played by a boy-actor whose voice is breaking.

"Aye, and he has a very imperfect face," Philautia said.

"Like a squeezed orange: sour, sour," Phantaste said.

Possibly, the boy-actor playing Anaides had acne.

"His hand's too great, too, by at least a straw's breadth," Philautia said.

A puppy's paws grow big before the rest of its body.

"He has a worse fault than that, too," Phantaste said.

"A long heel?" Philautia asked.

Phantaste said:

"That would be a fault in a lady rather than him."

The heel of the hand is the bottom of the palm. The heel pad is the fleshy part of the palm by the little finger.

According to a superstition, a man who has small hands also has a small penis. If Anaides has a long heel on his hand, he has a long penis.

Chances are, Phantaste was also talking about the heel of a foot.

According to a superstition, a man who has big feet also has a big penis.

Phantaste continued:

"No, they say he puts off the calves of his legs with his stockings every night."

In other words, his stockings are padded so that he will seem to have powerful calves.

"Bah to him!" Philautia said. "Turn to another of the pictures, for God's sake. What does Argurion say? Whom does she commend before the rest?"

Cupid said to himself, "I hope I have instructed her sufficiently for an answer."

Cupid had done what Cupid does: Make someone fall in love with someone else. In this case, he had made Argurion fall in love with Asotus.

Moria said, "Truly, I made the motion to her ladyship for one today in the presence, but it appeared she was other ways furnished before; she would none."

Moria had been trying to be a match-maker. She had been unsuccessful.

"Who was that, Argurion?" Phantaste asked.

"By the Virgin Mary, the little, poor, plain gentleman in the black there," Moria said.

Moria had wanted Argurion to fall in love with Criticus.

"Who, Criticus?" Phantaste asked.

"Aye, aye, he," Argurion said. "A fellow whom nobody so much as looked upon, or regarded, and she would have had me done him particular grace."

"That was a true trick of yourself, Moria, to persuade Argurion to affect and love the scholar," Phantaste said.

It really does seem sometimes that only Folly (Moria) could make Money (Argurion) fall in love with a Scholar (Criterion). Don't believe it? Ask a scholar if the scholar is wealthy.

"Tut, but she shall be no chooser for me," Argurion said. "In good faith, I like the citizen's son there, Asotus. I think none of the others come near him."

"Not Hedon?" Phantaste asked.

Argurion said:

"Hedon, indeed, no.

"Hedon's a pretty slight courtier, and he wears his clothes well and sometimes in fashion; by the Virgin Mary, his face is but indifferent, and he has no such excellent body.

"No, the other one — Asotus — is a most delicate youth, a sweet face, a straight body, a well-proportioned leg and foot, a white hand, a tender voice."

A white hand shows that Asotus does no outside work.

Asotus' late father is Philargyrus, whose name is derived from the Greek word for "money-lover."

Argurion's name, of course, means "Silver," aka "Money."

"How are things now, Argurion?" Philautia asked.

"Oh, you should have let her alone," Phantaste said. "She was bestowing a copy — a verbal portrait — of him upon us."

"Why, she dotes more palpably upon him than his father ever did upon her," Philautia said.

Phantaste said:

"Believe me, the young gentleman — Asotus — deserves it; if she could dote more, it would not be amiss. He is an exceedingly proper youth, and he would have made a most neat barber-surgeon, if he had been put to it in time."

Gentlemen were not barber-surgeons.

"Do you say so?" Philautia said. "I think he looks like a tailor already."

Gentlemen were not tailors.

"Aye, Asotus looks like a tailor who had assayed — tried — on one of his customers' suits," Phantaste said.

"Well, ladies, jest on," Argurion said. "The best of you both would be glad of such a servant — such a male admirer."

Moria said:

"Aye, I'll be sworn they would. Go on, beauties, make much of time, and place, and occasion, and opportunity, and favorites, and things that belong to them, for I'll ensure — assure — you that they will all relinquish and disappear; they cannot endure above another year.

"I know it out of future experience, and therefore take exhibition and warning: I was once a reveler myself, and although I am the one who says it, as my own trumpet, I was then esteemed —"

By her "future experience," which can be an oxymoron, Moria meant her own past experience of the then-future, which was now the past.

"Exhibition" can mean 1) display, and 2) financial support.

Philautia finished Moria's sentence: "— the very marchpane of the court, I say!"

"Marchpane" is the sweet treat known as marzipan.

"And all the gallants came about you like flies, didn't they?" Phantaste teased.

Moria said:

"Bah. They did somewhat, but that doesn't matter now.

"Here comes Hedon."

Hedon, Anaides, and Mercury entered the scene. Mercury was disguised as a page. He served Hedon.

Hedon said:

"God save you, sweet and clear beauties! By the spirit that moves in me, you are all most pleasingly bestowed, ladies. Only I can take it for no good omen to find my Honor so dejected."

Philautia called him "Ambition"; Hedon called her "Honor."

They were pet names.

"You need not fear, sir," Philautia said. "I did on purpose humble myself against your coming, to decline the pride of my Ambition."

Hedon replied, "Fair Honor, Ambition dares not stoop; but if it should be your sweet pleasure, I shall lose that title. I will, as I am Hedon, apply myself to your bounties."

"That would be the next way to distitle myself — take away the title — of Honor," Philautia said. "Oh, no, rather still be Ambition and ambitious, I ask you."

If Hedon ceased to be Ambition, Philautia would cease to be Honor.

Hedon replied:

"I will be anything that you please while it pleases you to be yourself, lady."

He then greeted the others:

"Sweet Phantaste, dear Moria, most beautiful Argurion —"

"Farewell, Hedon," Anaides said.

"Anaides, stay!" Hedon said. "Where are you going?"

"By God's light, what should I do here?" Anaides said. "If you engross them all for your own use, it is time for me to look elsewhere."

"Them all" means "all the ladies."

"Engross them all" can mean 1) take all their attention, or 2) buy all of them wholesale.

"I engross them?" Hedon said. "Away, mischief, this is one of your extravagant jests now because I began to salute and greet them by their names —"

Anaides said, "By my faith, you might have spared us Madam Prudence — Moria, the guardian there — although you had more covetously aimed at the rest."

"By God's heart, take them all, man!" Hedon said. "Why do you speak to me about aiming or being covetous?"

Anaides said:

"Aye, do you say so?

"Nay, then, I'll have a go at them.

"Ladies, here's one who has distinguished you by your names already. It shall only become me to ask, 'How do you do?'"

"By God's soul, was this the design you travailed with?" Hedon asked.

Was this his opening move with the ladies?

And earlier, he had shown a lack of couth when referring to Hedon's engrossing — buying — the ladies for his own use.

One meaning of "use" is "have sex with."

The ladies were silent until Phantaste said, "Who answers the brazen head? It spoke to somebody."

In legend, the magician Roger Bacon created a head out of bronze that spoke. Bacon was exhausted and so he was sleeping, and his foolish servant did not wake him up when the brazen head spoke. The Brazen Head spoke three times and was ignored each time, and then a supernatural hand destroyed it. Bacon had wanted the brazen head to tell him the secrets of the universe.

You can read the story in Robert Greene's play *Friar Bacon and Friar Bungay*.

Phantaste's point was that everyone was ignoring Anaides.

Anaides asked Moria, "Lady Wisdom, do you interpret — speak — for these puppets?"

He was calling the young ladies puppets because they were silent.

Moria chastised the young ladies:

"In truth and sadness, honors, you are in great offence for this. Bah!

"The gentleman (I'll undertake to speak up for him) is a man of fair living [a good income], and able to maintain a lady in her two coaches a day, besides pages, monkeys, and paraquitos [parakeets], with such attendants as she shall think fitting for her turn; and therefore there is more respect requirable, howsoever you seem to connive and take no notice of him."

Moria then chastised Anaides:

"Listen, sir, let me discourse a syllable with you. I am to say to you, these ladies are not of that close and open behavior as happily you may suspend."

Chances are, Moria was trying to say, "I am saying to you that these ladies are not of that secret [close] and open-legged behavior as perhaps you may suspect."

In other words, she was trying to say that these young ladies were not sexually promiscuous.

Moria continued:

"Their carriage is well known to be such as it should be, both gentle and extraordinary."

"Carriage" can mean 1) how a person moves his or her head and body, and 2) the act of carrying or bearing something.

A woman can bear the weight of a man in the missionary position.

Mercury said, "Oh, here comes the other pair."

Amorphus and Asotus entered the scene.

Amorphus said quietly to Asotus, "That woman was your father's love, the nymph Argurion. I would have you direct all your courtship toward her; if you could but endear yourself to her affection, you were eternally engallanted — made a gallant."

"Truly, sir?" Asotus said. "I pray to Phoebus Apollo that I prove favorsome — worthy of favor — in her fair eyes."

Amorphus said to those present, "I wish all divine mixture and increase of beauty to this bright bevy of ladies; and to the male courtiers, I wish compliment and courtesy!"

Hedon replied, "In the behalf of the males, I gratify — thank — you, Amorphus."

"And I of the females," Phantaste said.

Amorphus replied, "Succinctly spoken. I do vail — bow —to both your thanks and kiss them, but primarily to yours, most ingenious, acute, and polite lady."

He bowed and kissed Phantaste's hands.

Amorphus had greeted Phantaste first, and that made Philautia jealous.

Philautia said, "God's my life, how he does so much to bequalify — give qualities to — her! Ingenious, acute, and polite? As if there were not others in place as ingenious, acute, and polite as she!"

"Yes," Hedon said, "but you must know, lady, he cannot speak outside of a dictionary method."

Phantaste comes alphabetically before Philautia.

Phantaste said, "Sit down, sweet Amorphus. When will this water come, do you think?"

"It cannot now be long, fair lady," Amorphus said.

Cupid said quietly to Mercury, "Now observe, Mercury."

Asotus and Argurion had been speaking privately, and Argurion had just let him know she loved him and had given him permission to love her.

Asotus said to Argurion, "What, most ambiguous beauty, love you? That I will, I swear by this handkerchief."

Mercury said quietly to Cupid, "By God's eyelid, he draws his oaths out of his pocket."

"But will you be constant and loyal to me?" Argurion asked.

Asotus replied:

"Constant, madam? I will not say for constantness, but I swear by this purse — which I would be loath to swear by unless it were embroidered — I state, you more than most fair lady, that you are the only absolute and unparalleled creature I do adore, and admire, and respect, and reverence in this court, corner of the world, or kingdom.

"I think you are melancholy."

He was remembering Amorphus' advice in 3.5 to tell the woman he loved that he thought she was melancholy, but a woman who has just acquired a boyfriend ought not to be melancholy.

Actually, Amorphus had told him to say, "I think you are melancholy," only "if she be alone now and discompanied — without any company."

"Does your heart speak all this?" Argurion asked.

"What did you say?" Asotus asked.

Mercury said quietly to Cupid, "Oh, he is groping for another oath."

Asotus had not been listening to Argurion because he was trying to think of another oath.

Asotus said to Argurion:

"Now, by this watch —"

He said to himself:

"I marvel at how much forward and advanced the day is."

Asotus said to Argurion:

"— I do unfeignedly vow myself —"

He said to himself:

"By God's light, it is deeper and later than I took the time to be. It is past five."

Asotus said to Argurion:

"— yours entirely addicted — devoted, madam."

Argurion replied, "I require no more, dearest Asotus. Henceforth let me call you mine; and in remembrance of me, grant to me that you will wear this chain and this diamond."

A chain is a necklace.

She presented him with the gifts.

"Oh, God, sweet lady," Asotus said.

Cupid said quietly to Mercury:

"There are new oaths for him."

Now Asotus could swear by the chain and the diamond.

Cupid continued:

"Doesn't Hermes taste any alteration in all this?"

Mercury/Hermes said quietly to Cupid, "Yes, thou have struck Argurion enamored on Asotus, I think?"

Sarcastically, Cupid replied quietly, "Alas, no. I am nobody, I. I can do nothing in this disguise."

He was not carrying a bow and arrows, but he had an arrow hidden on him. Readers find out later that he need not shoot someone with an arrow to make them fall in love; he can just brandish — wave — an arrow at them.

Recognizing the sarcasm, Mercury then asked quietly, "But thou have not wounded any of the rest, Cupid?"

Cupid replied quietly, "Not yet; it is enough that I have begun so prosperously."

Argurion said to Asotus:

"Tut, these are nothing to the gems I will hourly bestow upon thee. Be but faithful and kind to me and I will lade — load — thee with my richest bounties.

"Behold, here, my bracelets from my arms."

She offered him her bracelets.

"It shall not be so, good lady, I swear by this diamond," Asotus said.

This was the diamond that she had just given to him.

Argurion said, "Take them; wear them; my jewels, chain of pearl, pendants, all I have."

Asotus said, "Then, I swear by this pearl, you make me a wanton — you spoil me."

This was one of the pearls in the chain — the necklace — she had just given to him.

Cupid whispered to Mercury, "Shall not she answer for this to maintain him thus in swearing?"

Asotus was swearing with each gift she gave him.

Mercury whispered to Cupid, "Oh, no, there is a way to wean him from this. The gentleman may be reclaimed."

In other words, the gentleman may be made to not swear by her gifts.

Cupid whispered to Mercury, "Aye, if you had the airing of his apparel, coz, I think."

Clothes were washed and then left in the air to dry. Thieves often stole drying clothing.

Mercury was a thief, and if he stole Asotus' clothing, then Asotus would have no pockets to put Argurion's gifts in and so Asotus would have no gifts to swear by.

In addition, since Mercury was a thief, if he stole the gifts that Argurion was giving to Asotus, then Asotus would have no gifts to swear by.

Argurion had just asked, quietly, whether Asotus would be loving to her.

Asotus replied, "Loving? It would be a pity I should be living if I were not loving to you, believe me."

He said to Hedon, "God save you, sir."

He then said:

"God save you, sweet lady.

"God save you, Monsieur Anaides.

"God save you, dear madam."

Anaides asked, "Do thou know the man who saluted thee, Hedon?"

Hedon replied, "No, he is some idle *fungoso*, I promise you."

A *fungoso* is a mushroom. The word was used for someone who seemed to rise high in society overnight.

"By God's blood, I never saw him until this morning, and he greets me as familiarly as if we had known each other since the first year of the siege of Troy," Anaides said.

The traditional date of the fall of Troy is 1184 B.C.E. Since the Trojan War lasted for 10 years, the first year of the siege was 1194 B.C.E.

Amorphus said, "A most right-handed and auspicious encounter. Confine yourself to your fortunes."

The Latin word *sinister* means "left." A right-handed encounter is a fortunate encounter.

Philautia proposed that they play a game while waiting for the water from the fountain to arrive: "For God's sake, let's have some riddles or purposes!"

In the game of purposes, each player whispers a question to the person who is next to him or her, and that person comes up with an answer. Then a question and an answer are stated out loud, but in such an order that the questions and the answers are not asked and answered in the correct order, so that the answers are at cross-purposes, often amusingly so, with the questions.

Phantaste said, "No, indeed, your prophecies are the best game; the other games are stale."

Possibly, the game of prophecies was talked about in 2.2 when Hedon said, "I have ruminated upon a most rare — splendid — wish, too, and the prophecy to it, but I'll have some friend to be the prophet, as thus: 'I wish that I were one of my mistress' *ciopinos*.'"

Philautia said:

"Prophecies? We cannot all sit in at them; we shall make a confusion.

"No, what did you call that game we played in the forenoon — the morning?"

"Substantives and adjectives," Phantaste said. "Isn't that right, Hedon?"

Substantives are nouns.

"I say aye to that game," Philautia said. "Who begins?"

"I have thought of a substantive," Phantaste said. "Speak your adjectives, sirs."

"But don't you change your substantive, then," Philautia said.

"I won't," Phantaste said. "Who says the first adjective?"

"Odoriferous," Moria said.

"Popular," Philautia said.

"Humble," Argurion said.

"White-livered," Anaides said.

"Barbarous," Hedon said.

"Pythagorical," Amorphus said.

Hedon said to Asotus, "It's your turn, signor."

"What must I do, sir?" Asotus asked.

Amorphus answered, "Give forth your adjective with the rest; for example, prosperous, good, fair, sweet, well."

Hedon added, "Any adjective that has not been spoken previously."

"Yes, sir, 'well-spoken' shall be my adjective," Asotus said.

"Have you all done?" Phantaste asked.

All answered, "Aye."

Phantaste said:

"Then the substantive is 'breeches.'

She asked Moria:

"Why *odoriferous* breeches, guardian?"

The game was for a player to silently think of a noun and for the other players to name out loud an adjective each. The first player then announces what the noun is, and the other players explain how their adjective modifies that noun.

Moria answered:

"Odoriferous, because odoriferous: That which contains most variety of savor and smell, we say is most odoriferous.

"Now, breeches I presume are incident to that variety, and therefore, odoriferous breeches."

Breeches can smell differently before and after being washed. They can also smell differently if given to someone else who wears them. A fart can make breeches smell differently.

"Well, we must take it howsoever we can," Phantaste said. "Who's next? Philautia."

Philautia said, "My adjective is 'popular.'"

"Popular" can mean "common, or popular with commoners." It can mean "not noble" and "vulgar." An antonym of "popular" is "highbrow."

Phantaste asked, "Why *popular* breeches?"

Philautia answered, "By the Virgin Mary, that is when they are not content to be generally noted in court, but will press forth on common stages and brokers' stalls to the public view of the world."

Common stages do not include Blackfriars, where this play by Ben Jonson was performed. Blackfriars was a private theater.

Brokers' stalls are second-hand stalls.

"Good," Phantaste said. "Why *humble* breeches, Argurion?"

Argurion answered, "They are humble, because they are accustomed to be sat upon. Besides, if you don't tie them up, their property is to fall down about your heels."

Having one's breeches fall down in public can be a humbling experience.

Mercury said quietly to Cupid, "She has worn the breeches, it seems, which have done so."

Mercury was joking that at some time Argurion had worn pants that had fallen down.

Some women wear the breeches in a relationship.

"But why *white-livered*?" Phantaste asked.

Anaides said:

"Why? By God's heart, aren't their linings white?"

Breeches can have white linings.

Anaides added:

"Besides, when they come in swaggering company, and will pocket up anything, may they not properly be said to be white-livered?"

Swaggerers were bullies, and their insults could be pocketed — cowardly endured. White-livered (or lily-livered) people were cowards.

Phantaste said:

"Oh, yes, we cannot deny it.

"And why *barbarous*, Hedon?"

Hedon answered, "Barbarous, because commonly when you have worn your breeches sufficiently, you give them to your barber."

"That's good," Amorphus said. "But now *Pythagorical*."

Pythagoras was a Greek philosopher who believed in reincarnation: the transmigration of souls from one body into another.

"Aye, Amorphus," Phantaste said. "Why *Pythagorical* breeches?"

"Oh, most kindly of all, it is a conceit of that fortune I am bold to hug my brain for," Amorphus said.

"What conceit — idea — is it, exquisite Amorphus?" Phantaste asked.

"Oh, I am rapt with it," Amorphus said. "It is so fit, so proper, so happy."

"Nay, do not rack us thus!" Philautia said.

In other words: Don't torture us with anticipation.

Amorphus said, "I never truly relished myself before. Give me your ears: breeches are Pythagorical, by reason of their transmigration into several shapes!"

Different people could wear the breeches — the gallant first and then his barber — and so the breeches were transmigrated from one body into another. Since bodies differ, and clothes stretch and adapt to suit the wearer (clothes are more comfortable after they have been worn a few times), the trousers can transmigrate into different shapes.

"Most splendid, in sweet truth!" Moria said. "By the Virgin Mary, this young gentleman, for his well-spoken —"

Phantaste interrupted, "Aye — why *well-spoken* breeches?"

"Well-spoken?" Asotus said. "By the Virgin Mary, well-spoken because whatsoever they speak is well taken, and whatsoever is well taken, is well-spoken."

Breeches speak when their wearer farts, and listeners tend to laugh. Laughter is good, and so the breeches are well-taken.

Breeches can also speak by proclaiming the wearer's social class. Gentlemen wear clothing different — better quality and more expensive — from the clothing farmers wear.

"This is excellent, believe me," Moria said.

"Not so, ladies, neither," Asotus said, modestly.

"But why breeches now?" Hedon asked.

Phantaste answered, "Breeches, quasi — as if — bear-riches; when a gallant bears all his riches in his breeches."

Asotus had placed Argurion's gifts to him in his breeches' pockets.

Changing the subject, Philautia said, "In good faith, these unhappy pages would be — ought to be — whipped for staying away thus long."

The pages were the people who had gone to get water from the fountain. They were taking a long time.

"Curse my hand and my heart else," Moria said.

"I do wonder at their protracted absence," Amorphus said.

"I pray to God that my whore has not discovered — revealed — herself to the rascally boys, and that is the reason of their stay and delay," Anaides said.

His "whore" was Gelaia, a woman dressed in the clothing of a page. The boys were Prosaites and Cos. They were the pages bringing back the water.

"I must suit myself with another page," Asotus said. "This idle Prosaites will never be brought to wait well."

"Sir, I have a kinsman I could willingly wish to your service, if you would deign to accept him to your service," Moria said.

She was talking about her relative becoming Asotus' page.

"And I shall be glad, most sweet lady, to embrace him," Asotus said. "Where is he?"

"I can fetch him, sir, but I would be loath to make you turn away and fire your other page," Moria said.

"You shall not, most sufficient lady. I will keep them both employed as my pages," Asotus said. "Please, let's go and see him."

"Whither goes my love?" Argurion asked Asotus.

"I'll return soon," Asotus said. "I am going just to see a page with this lady."

Asotus and Moria exited.

Anaides said about Gelaia, his page:

"As sure as fate, it is so. She has opened all — a pox on all cockatrices!"

"Cockatrices" are literally monsters that are also known as basilisks. They are figuratively prostitutes.

"Opened all" means 1) revealed all, and 2) opened both legs.

Anaides continued:

"Damn me if she has played loose with me. I'll cut her throat within a hair's breadth, so it may be healed again."

Anaides was threatening to cut the skin of her throat, but he would not kill her.

He exited.

Mercury said quietly to Cupid, "What, is he jealous of his hermaphrodite?"

Anaides' "hermaphrodite" was Gelaia, who served Anaides as a page. She was female, but she was dressed as a male page.

Cupid whispered back, "Oh, aye, this will be excellent entertainment."

Philautia said:

"Phantaste, Argurion, what? You are sudden struck, I think."

"Struck" may be 1) wonderstruck, 2) struck silent, or 3) struck ill.

Philautia continued:

"For God's will, let's have some music until they come back with the water.

"Ambition, hand me the lyra, please."

Hedon said as he handed her a harp, "Anything to which my Honor shall direct me."

Philautia then said, "Come, Amorphus, cheer up Phantaste."

Earlier, Amorphus had greeted Phantaste before he had greeted Philautia.

Amorphus said:

"It shall be my pride, fair lady, to attempt all that is in my power.

"But here is an instrument that alone is able to infuse soul in the most melancholic and dull-disposed creature upon Earth.

"Oh, let me kiss thy fair knees!"

A knee can be an angular piece of wood, so he may be saying that he wanted to kiss the wooden musical instrument.

Amorphus asked Philautia:

Will you have 'The Kiss,' Honor?"

Philautia answered, "Aye, good Ambition."

Hedon sang "The Kiss":

"*Oh, that joy so soon should waste!*

"*Or so sweet a bliss*

"*As a kiss,*

"*Might not forever last!*

"*So sugared, so melting, so soft, so delicious,*

"*The dew that lies on roses,*

"*When the morn herself discloses [discloses herself],*

"*Is not so precious.*

"*Oh, rather than I would it smother,*

"*Were I to taste such another;*

"*It should be my wishing*

"*That I might die kissing.*"

Hedon then said:

"I made this ditty and the musical notes to it about a kiss that my Honor gave me.

"How do you like it, sir?"

Amorphus answered, "It is a pretty air! In general, I like it well. But, in particular, your long 'die' note did arride — gratify — me most, but it was somewhat too long. I can show one almost of the same nature but much before it, and not so long, in a composition of my own. I think I have both the note and ditty about me."

The "die" note is the note on which the word "die" is sung.

Hedon said, "Sir, see if you have it."

Amorphus produced a paper and said:

"Yes, there is the note and all the parts, if I am not misthinking — mistaken.

"I will read the ditty to your beauties here, but first I will make you familiar with the occasion, which presents itself thus:

"Once upon a time, going to take my leave of the Emperor and kiss his great hands, there being then present the Kings of France and Aragon, the Dukes of Savoy, Florence, Orleans, Bourbon, Brunswick, the Landgrave, Count Palatine — all of which had individually feasted me — besides an infinite number more of inferior persons, such as Earls and others — it was my chance, the Emperor being detained by some other affair, to wait for him the fifth part of an hour, or much near it.

"In which time, retiring myself into a bay-window, I encountered the Lady Annabel, niece to the Empress and sister to the King of Aragon, who, having never before eyed me but only heard the common report of my virtue, learning, and travel, fell into that extremity of passion for my love that she there immediately sounded — that is, swooned — that is, fainted.

"Physicians were sent for; she had recourse to her chamber; so to her bed, where languishing some few days, after many times calling upon me, with my name in her mouth, she expired and died.

"As that, I must necessarily say, is the only fault of my fortune, that as it has always been my hap — my luck — to be sued to by all ladies and beauties where I have come, so I never yet sojourned or rested in that place or part of the world where some great and admirable fair creature did not die for my love — die out of love for me."

Mercury said quietly to Cupid, "Oh, the sweet power of travel! Are you guilty of this, Cupid?"

Cupid quietly replied, "No, Mercury; and that his page, Cos, knows, if he were here present to be sworn."

In other words, Amorphus was lying.

Philautia asked Amorphus, "But how does this draw on the ditty, sir? What does it have to do with the story?"

Mercury said quietly to Cupid, "Oh, she is too quick with him. He has not devised an answer for that yet."

Mercury was wrong.

Amorphus said to Philautia, "By the Virgin Mary, some hour before she departed, she bequeathed to me this glove" — he displayed the glove — "which the Emperor himself took care to send after me, in six coaches, covered all with black velvet, attended by the stately principal people of his empire; all of which he freely gave me, and I reciprocally (out of the same bounty) gave it to the lords who brought it; only reserving, and respecting, this glove — the gift of the deceased lady — upon which I composed this ode, and set it to my most affected — loved — instrument, the lyra."

Amorphus read out loud the lyrics to his song about a lady's glove:

"*Thou more than most sweet glove,*

"*Unto my more sweet love,*

"*Suffer [Allow] me to store with kisses*

"*This empty lodging, that now misses*

"*The pure rosy hand that ware [wore] thee,*

"*Whiter than the kid [baby goat] that bare [bore] thee.*

"*Thou art [are] soft, but that was softer;*

"*Cupid's self hath [has] kissed it ofter [oftener],*

"*Than e'er [ever] he did his mother's doves,*

"*Supposing her the Queen of Love's,*

"*That [Who] was thy mistress,*

"*Best of gloves.*"

Doves were sacred to Venus: They pulled her chariot, sometimes assisted by swans.

Mercury said to Cupid, "Blasphemy, blasphemy, Cupid!"

Amorphus had said that Cupid had kissed the lady's glove more often than he had ever kissed his mother's doves.

Cupid replied quietly, "Aye, I'll revenge it time — soon — enough, Hermes."

"Good Amorphus, let's hear it sung," Philautia requested.

"I am not concerned negatively about doing that, since it pleases Philautia to request it," Amorphus said.

"Here, sir," Hedon said, offering him the harp.

"Nay, you play it, please," Amorphus said, declining to take the harp. "You do well, you do well."

Amorphus sang his lyrics while Hedon played.

Amorphus then asked, "How do you like it, sir?"

"Very well, indeed," Hedon said.

Amorphus said:

"Only 'very well'? Oh, you are a mere mammothrept in judgment then!"

"Mammothrept" can mean 1) a spoiled child, or 2) a severe critic.

Amorphus continued:

"Why, don't you observe how excellently the ditty is affected — good — in every place?

"Don't you observe that I do not marry a word of short quantity [time] to a long note, nor an ascending syllable to a descending tone?

"Besides, upon the word 'best' there, you see how I do enter with an odd minim and drive it through the breve, which no intelligent musician I know but will affirm to be very rare, extraordinary, and pleasing."

Quantity [time] can be long or short.

A breve is a musical note four times the length of a minim.

One wonders how Hedon could play the tune: He must have practiced it ahead of time. Amorphus must have planned to sing the song to the ladies at some time.

Amorphus' criticism of Hedon is unjustified because Hedon had helped him by playing the harp.

Mercury said quietly to Cupid, "And yet the song is not fit to lament the death of a lady for all this."

As the inventor of the harp, Mercury has some knowledge of music.

Cupid replied quietly, "Tut, here are people who will swallow anything."

"Please, let me have a copy of it, Amorphus," Phantaste requested.

"And me, too," Philautia requested. "Indeed, I like it exceedingly."

"I have denied it to princes; nevertheless, to you, the true female twins of perfection, I am won over to depart with it," Amorphus said.

Amorphus gave sheets of paper containing the lyrics to Philautia and Phantaste.

He was prepared to give away copies of the song: This was more evidence that the song's performance was pre-planned.

"I hope I shall have my Honor's [Philautia's] copy," Hedon said.

"You are ambitious in that, Hedon," Phantaste said.

Hedon was Ambition to Philautia's Honor.

Anaides entered the scene. He seemed upset.

"How are you now, Anaides?" Amorphus asked. "What is it that has conjured up this distemperature in the circle of your face?"

"By God's blood, what have you to do with it?" Anaides said. "A pox of God on your filthy travelling beard! Hold your tongue."

"Have you heard some evil?" Hedon asked Anaides.

"Go away, musk-cat!" Anaides said.

Musk-cats stank, although their musk was made into perfume. Sometimes, wearing too much perfume makes a person stink.

"I say to thee, thou are rude, impudent, coarse, impolished, aka unpolished or badly polished; a frapler, and base," Amorphus said.

A frapler is a blusterer.

Hedon said to himself, "By the heart of my father, what a strange alteration has half a year's haunting of ordinaries wrought in this fellow! He came with a tuftaffeta jacket to town just the other day, and now he has turned into Hercules; he lacks only a club!"

Tuftaffeta is tufted taffeta.

The great PanHellenic hero Hercules carried a club.

"Sir, I will garter my hose with your guts and that shall be all," Anaides said.

He exited.

Mercury said quietly to Cupid, "By God's eyelid, what splendid fireworks are here? Flash! Flash!"

"What's the matter with Anaides, Hedon?" Phantaste asked. "Can you tell?"

Hedon replied, "I can guess nothing except that he lacks money, and he thinks we'll lend him some to be friends."

Asotus, Moria, and Morus entered the scene.

The name "Morus" means "Simpleton.'

He was Moria's nephew, and Asotus had just hired him to be his second page.

Asotus, who had asked Moria for her picture and had given her a gift and had made promises to her, said to her:

"Come, sweet lady, in good truth I'll have it, you shall not deny me."

He then said:

"Morus, persuade your aunt to give me her picture, by any means necessary."

Morus said:

"Yes, sir."

He then said to Moria:

"Good aunt, now, let him have it. He will treat me the better, so if you love me, do give him your picture, good aunt."

"Well, tell him he shall have it," Moria said.

Morus said to Asotus, "Master, you shall have it, she says."

"Shall I?" Asotus said. "Thank her, good page."

Cupid whispered to Mercury, "What, has he entertained — hired — the fool?"

Mercury whispered back, "Aye, he'll wait close by him, you shall see, although the beggar — Prosaites — hang off at a distance."

Morus said to Moria, "Aunt, my master thanks you."

"Call him to come here," Moria said.

"Yes," Morus said.

He then called, "Master!"

Moria said, "Yes, in very truth, and he gave me this purse, and he has promised me a most fine dog that he will have drawn with my picture, and he desires most vehemently to be known to Your Ladyships."

Moria liked dogs.

Phantaste said, "Call him to come here; it is good groping — examining and exploiting — such a gull."

A gull is a fool.

Moria called, "Master Asotus! Master Asotus!"

Asotus said to Argurion, who loved him, "For God's sake, let me go. You see I am called to the ladies."

"Will thou forsake me, then?" Argurion asked.

"By God's soul, what would you have me do?" Asotus asked.

Moria called:

"Come here, Master Asotus."

She then said to the ladies:

"I do ensure — assure — Your Ladyships that he is a gentleman of a very worthy desert and of a most bountiful nature."

Moria said to Asotus:

"You must show and insinuate yourself responsible and equivalent now to my commendment."

She then said to the ladies:

"Good honors, grace him."

Asotus recited part of a speech he had practiced with Amorphus in 3.5:

"I protest, more than most fair ladies, I do wish all variety of divine pleasure, choice entertainment, sweet music, rich fare, brave attires, soft beds, and silken thoughts attend these fair beauties."

Asotus then said to Phantaste:

"Will it please Your Ladyship to wear this chain of pearl, and this diamond for my sake?"

He presented her with the pearl necklace and diamond that Argurion had given to him earlier to remember her by.

"Oh!" Argurion said.

Asotus then said to Philautia:

"And I present to you, madam, this jewel and pendants."

He presented her with a jewel and some pendants that Argurion had given to him earlier to remember her by.

"Oh!" Argurion said.

Phantaste said, "We don't know how to deserve these bounties out of so slight merit, Asotus."

Who has the slight merit? The ladies? Asotus? Both?

"No, indeed, but there's my glove for a favor," Philautia said.

She offered him a glove.

"And soon after the revels I will bestow a garter on you," Phantaste said.

Asotus replied:

"Oh, Lord, ladies, it is more grace than ever I could have hoped, but that it pleases Your Ladyships to extend. I protest it is enough that you just take knowledge of my — if Your Ladyships want embroidered gowns, tires [headdresses] of any fashion, rebatoes [stiff collars], jewels, or carcanets [ornamental collars or necklaces], anything whatsoever, if you vouchsafe to accept."

Hmm. To "just take knowledge of my —" The Bible sometimes mentions a particular kind of knowledge.

Cupid whispered to Mercury, "And for it they will help you to shoe-ties and devices."

Asotus was giving the ladies big gifts such as pearls and diamonds, and they were giving him the small gift of a glove and the promise of a small gift of a garter.

A shoe-tie is a ribbon to be worn as a decoration on shoes.

"Devices" are tricks.

Asotus said, "I cannot express myself well, dear beauties, but you can conceive —"

Yes, they can become pregnant.

"Oh!" Argurion said.

"Sir, we will acknowledge your service, fear not," Phantaste said. "Henceforth, you shall be no more 'Asotus' to us but our goldfinch, and we shall be your cages."

The word "finch" can mean "fool." Asotus is their gold-finch: a fool who gives his gold away.

"Oh, God, madams, how shall I deserve this?" Asotus said.

He then said to himself:

"If I were only made acquainted with Hedon now! I'll try."

He said to Argurion, who loved him, "Please, go away."

Mercury whispered to Cupid, "How he prays Money to go away from him!"

Asotus said quietly, "Amorphus, let me have a word with you. Here's a watch I would bestow upon you. Please make me known to that gallant."

Amorphus said quietly, "That I will, sir."

He then said out loud, "Monsieur Hedon, I must entreat you to exchange knowledge with this gentleman."

To exchange knowledge meant to get to know each other.

"It is a thing, next to the water we expect, I thirst after, sir. Good Monsieur Asotus," Hedon said.

Asotus said:

"Good Monsieur Hedon, I would be glad to be loved and respected by men of your rank and spirit, I declare.

"Please accept this pair of bracelets, sir; they are not worth the bestowing."

The bracelets were those Argurion had earlier given to him.

Asotus offered Hedon the gifts.

Mercury whispered to Cupid, "Oh, Hercules, how the gentleman purchases! This must necessarily bring Argurion to a consumption."

Cupid had much power, as did Hercules. He had made Argurion love Asotus, and now Argurion was suffering because of her love for Asotus.

Asotus was attempting to purchase friends.

Ironically, the phrase "to purchase" at this time also meant "to become rich," Asotus was becoming poorer, but his "friends" were becoming richer.

Consumption is a wasting-away disease.

Argurion — Money — was wasting away because Asotus was giving away all the wealth that she had given to him to remember her by.

"Sir, I shall never stand in the merit of such bounty, I fear," Hedon said.

In other words, he did not deserve such valuable gifts.

Asotus replied, "Oh, Lord, sir, your acquaintance shall be sufficient. And if at any time you need my bill or my bond —"

He was willing to make legal agreements that could result in his paying the expenses and debts of a man to whom he had just been introduced: Hedon.

"Oh! Oh!" Argurion said.

She fainted.

"Help the lady there!" Amorphus said.

"God's dear, Argurion!" Moria said. "Madam, how are you?"

"Sick," Argurion said.

"Take her forth and give her air," Phantaste said.

"I will come back again straightaway, ladies," Asotus said.

Mercury whispered to Cupid, "Well, I doubt all the physic — medicine — he has will scarcely recover her; she's too far spent."

Asotus and Morus helped Argurion to leave the scene.

Anaides, Gelaia, Cos, and Prosaites entered the scene. They were carrying bottles filled with water from the Fountain of Self-Love. Anaides and Gelaia had been arguing.

Philautia said:

"Oh, here's the water come.

"Fetch some glasses, page."

Gelaia said to Anaides, "Heart of my body, here's a coil — a fuss — indeed with your jealous humors and moods. Nothing but 'whore,' and 'bitch,' and all the villainous swaggering names you can think of to call me! By God's eyelid, take your bottle and put it in your guts for all I care, I'll see you poxed — infected with syphilis — before I follow you any longer!"

One way for Anaides to put his bottle in his guts would be for him to stick it up his —

"Nay, good punk, sweet rascal," Anaides said. "Damn me if I am jealous now."

A "punk" is a prostitute, but Anaides may now be using the word affectionately.

"That's true indeed," Gelaia said.

She then said, "Please, let's go."

To whom was she speaking? Anaides? Or Moria?

"What's the matter there?" asked Moria, who was Gelaia's mother.

Gelaia replied, "By God's light, he has me upon interrogatories — he keeps asking me questions."

She said to Anaides, "Nay, my mother shall know how you treat me."

She said to her mother, "He asks where I have been? And why I should stay so long? And how is it possible? And in addition he calls me at his pleasure I don't know how many cockatrices and things."

"Cockatrices" are prostitutes.

Moria said, "In truth and sadness, these are no good epithets, Anaides, to bestow upon any gentlewoman; and, I'll ensure — assure — you, if I had known you would have dealt thus with my daughter, she should never have fancied you as deeply as she has done. Go to!"

Go to where? Hell?

"Why, do you hear, Mother Moria?" Anaides said. "By God's heart!"

"Nay, please, sir, do not swear," Moria said.

Anaides replied, "Swear? Why, by God's blood, I have sworn before now, I hope. Both you and your daughter mistake me. I have not honored Arete, who is held the worthiest lady in the court (next to Cynthia), with half that observance and respect as I have done her in private, howsoever outwardly I have carried myself careless — without cares and worries — and negligent."

He then said to Gelaia, "Come, you are a foolish punk and don't know when you are well employed. Kiss me. Come on. Do it, I say!"

Moria said, "Nay, indeed I must confess that Gelaia is apt to misprision — misapprehension and misunderstanding."

She then said to Anaides, "But I must have you stop what you are doing, minion."

The meaning of the word "minion" can be good or bad. The word can mean "darling" or "favorite," or it can mean "slave" or "underling."

Asotus entered the scene.

Seeing him, Amorphus asked, "How are you now, Asotus? How is the lady Argurion doing?"

"Indeed, she is ill," Asotus said. "I have left my page with her at her lodging."

His page was Morus, who had helped him assist Argurion.

Hedon drank some of the water.

"Oh, here's the rarest and most splendid water that ever was tasted," Hedon said.

He then said to Prosaites, Asotus' first page, "Fill a glass with some water for him."

The water was for Asotus.

Prosaites whispered to Mercury, "What? Has my master a new page?"

Mercury whispered back, "Yes, a kinsman of the Lady Moria's. You must serve your master better now or you are cashiered — fired, Prosaites."

"Come, gallants, you must pardon my foolish humor," Anaides said. "When I am angry that anything crosses me, I grow impatient straightaway. Here, I drink to you."

He drank.

Philautia said, "Oh, I wish that we had five or six bottles more of this liquor!"

"Now, I commend your judgment, Amorphus," Phantaste said.

A knock sounded on the door.

Phantaste asked, "Who's that who is knocking? Go and see, page."

Cupid went to the door.

"Oh, this water is most delicious!" Moria said. "A little of this would make Argurion well."

Phantaste said, "Oh, no, give her no cold drink, by any means."

"'Slud — by God's blood, this water is the spirit of wine — I'll be hanged if it isn't," Anaides said.

All the courtiers present — male and female — had drunk the water.

"Here's the Lady Arete, madam," Cupid said.

Arete entered the scene.

"What, at your beverages, gallants?" Arete said.

"Will it please Your Ladyship to drink?" Moria asked. "It is water from the new fountain."

The new fountain was, of course, the Fountain of Self-Love.

Arete, whose name means "Virtue" and "Excellence," said:

"Not I, Moria, I thank you.

"Gallants, you must provide some solemn — ceremonial — revels tonight. Cynthia is minded to come forth and grace your entertainments with her presence.

"Therefore, I could wish there were something extraordinary to entertain her."

"What do you say to a masque?" Amorphus asked.

A masque is an informal court entertainment such as a dance with the dancers wearing masks. Or it could be an allegorical tableau in which the allegorical characters wear masks. Or both.

Hedon said, "Nothing is better, if the invention or project is new and splendid."

"Why, I'll send for Criticus and have his advice," Arete said.

She said to Phantaste, "You will be ready in your endeavors?"

"Yes, but won't Your Ladyship stay for a while?" Phantaste asked.

"Not now, Phantaste," Arete said.

She exited.

"Let her go, please," Philautia said. "That good Lady Sobriety, I am glad we are rid of her."

All too often, Virtue and Excellence are not liked and respected.

"What a set face the gentlewoman has, as if she were always going to a sacrifice!" Phantaste said.

"Oh, she is the extraction of a dozen of Puritans for a look," Philautia said.

"Of all nymphs in the court I cannot tolerate her; it is the coarsest thing —" Moria said.

Arete and Moria — Virtue/Excellence and Folly — do not go together.

Philautia said, "I wonder how Cynthia can love her so above the rest! Here are nymphs who are in every way as fair as she, and a thought fairer, I am sure."

"Aye, and as ingenious and conceited — filled with conceits, aka ideas — as she," Phantaste said.

"Aye, and as politic as she, for all she sets such a forehead on it," Moria said. "She makes a show that she is opposed to it."

Politic people scheme to get their way.

"I would wish I were dead if I would change to be Cynthia!" Philautia said.

One must be filled with Self-Love to not want to be more like Cynthia — or like Arete.

"Or I," Phantaste said

"Or I," Moria said.

Phantaste and Moria were saying that they also would wish to be dead if they would change to be Cynthia, but it sounded as if they were saying that Philautia would wish she were dead if she would change to be more like them.

Amorphus said, "And there's her minion — her darling — Criticus; why is his advice worth more than Amorphus' advice? Haven't I invention before him? Learning, to better that invention, above him? And travail —"

Anaides interrupted:

"— by Death, why are you talking about his 'learning'? He understands no more than a schoolboy.

"I have put him down myself a thousand times, I swear by this air, and yet I never talked with him but twice in my life.

"You never saw his like; I could never get him to argue with me but once, and then, because I could not construe a piece of Horace at first sight, he went away and laughed at me.

"By God's will, I scorn him, as I do the sodden nymph who was here just now, his mistress Arete, and I love myself for nothing else."

Apparently, Criticus declines to argue with Anaides because he does not respect Anaides.

Hedon said, "I wonder why the fellow does not hang himself, being thus scorned and contemned — regarded with contempt — by us who are held the most accomplished society of gallants!"

Mercury whispered to Cupid, "That is, 'held the most accomplished society of gallants' by themselves, and by no one else."

Hedon said, "I declare, if I had no music in me, no courtship, if I were not a reveler and could dance, or had not those excellent qualities that give a man life and perfection, but instead I were a mere poor scholar as he is, I think I should make some desperate way — and make away — with myself; whereas now, I wish that I might never breathe more if I do know that creature in this kingdom with whom I would exchange selves."

Hedon so loved himself that he wished to be no other person than himself. The same was true of all the others who drank water from the Fountain of Self-Love. No wonder none of the ladies liked Arete or wished to be Cynthia.

One characteristic of Self-Love is looking down on other people.

Self-Love is different from Proper Pride, which is pride of oneself that is reasonable and justifiable.

Proper Pride builds oneself up by doing things to be proud of; Self-Love builds oneself up by tearing others down.

Cupid whispered to Mercury, "This is excellent entertainment! Well, I must alter this soon."

Mercury whispered back, "Be sure that you do, Cupid."

Asotus said:

"Oh, I shall tickle it soon. I did never appear until then. By God's eyelid, I am the neatliest-made gallant in the company and have the best presence; and my dancing — I know what the usher said to me the last time I was at the school.

"I wish that I might lead Philautia in the measure, if it would be God's will! I am most worthy, I am sure."

Morus, Asotus' new page, entered the scene and said, "Master, I can tell you news: The lady kissed me yonder, and played with me, and says she loved you once as well as she does me, but that you cast her off."

Fortune favors fools.

The lady was Argurion.

"Peace, my most esteemed page," Asotus said. "Be quiet."

"Yes," Morus said.

Amorphus said, "Gallants, think upon your time, and take it by the forehead."

Time (and opportunity) must be seized by the forelock; she is bald except for the forelock. Once time (and opportunity) have passed by you, you cannot seize them.

Amorphus then said, "Anaides, we must mix this gentleman with you in acquaintance, Monsieur Asotus."

Anaides said, "I am easily entreated to grace any of your friends, Amorphus."

"Sir, and his friends shall likewise grace you, sir," Asotus said. "Nay, I begin to know myself now."

"To know thyself" is something good, but one can wonder whether Asotus really knows himself.

Amorphus whispered to Asotus, "Oh, you must continue your bounties."

In other words: You must continue to give away valuable items.

Asotus whispered back, "Must I? Why, I'll give him this ruby on my finger."

"Come, ladies," Hedon said. "But wait, we shall want one to lady it — act as a lady — in our masque in place of Argurion."

"Why, my page — Gelaia — shall do it," Anaides said.

"In truth, and he'll do it well," Hedon said. "It shall be so."

Hedon apparently did not know that Gelaia was a young woman dressed in the clothing of a page.

Hedon, Phantaste, Philautia, Moria, Gelaia, and Amorphus exited.

Asotus said to Anaides, "Do you hear, sir? I heartily wish your acquaintance, and I partly know myself worthy of it. Please you, sir, to accept this poor ruby in a ring, sir. The poesy is of my own device: 'Let this blush for me,' sir."

Asotus offered him a ruby ring.

"So it must blush for me, too," Anaides said. "For I am not ashamed to take it."

He took the ruby ring and exited.

Morus said:

"Sweet man, by my truth, master, I love you; will you love me, too, for my aunt's sake? I'll serve you well, you shall see, I'll still be here."

"I wish I might never stir, but you are in gay clothes."

Morus wanted Asotus' clothes as a gift.

"As for that, Morus, thou shall see more hereafter," Asotus said.

Perhaps Asotus was planning to strip off his clothes later so he could give them away.

He looked in his pockets, found nothing of value — he had given much or all of his wealth away — and said, "In the meantime, by this air, or by this feather, I'll do as much for thee as any gallant shall do for his page whatsoever, 'in this court, corner of the world, or kingdom.'"

Everyone except for the pages — Mercury, Cupid, Prosaites, Cos, and Morus — exited.

Mercury said, "I marvel that this gentleman Asotus should affect to keep a fool; I think he makes entertainment enough with himself."

Some fools, aka Fools, are jesters. Other fools are fools.

Cupid said, "Well, Prosaites, it would be good if you waited closer at hand to your master."

"Aye, I'll look to it," Prosaites said. "It is time."

"We are likely to have sumptuous revels tonight, sirs," Cos said.

Mercury said, "We must necessarily have sumptuous revels, when all the choicest singularities — the most notable people — of the court are up in pantofles; never a one of them but is able to make a whole show of itself."

"Up in pantofles" can mean 1) standing on shoes with thick, built-up soles, or 2) standing on one's dignity.

Hedon called from another room, "Sirrah, a torch! A torch!"

"Oh, what a call is there!" Mercury said. "I will have a canzonet — a short song — made with nothing in it but 'sirrah'; and the burden — the refrain — shall be 'I am coming.'"

Everyone exited.

Arete and Criticus talked together about the masque. They were virtuous courtiers who were not guilty of Self-Love.

Criticus, who opposed having the masque, said:

"A masque, bright Arete?

"Why, it would be a labor more for Hercules.

"Better and sooner would I dare undertake to make the different seasons of the year, the winds, or the elements to sympathize, than undertake to make their (the self-loving courtiers') unmeasurable (that is, immeasurable, and unable to dance the measures of songs) vanity dance truly in a measure.

"They agree?

"So what if all concord is borne of contraries? So many follies will prove to be confusion and destruction, and like a group of jarring instruments, all out of tune.

"Why? Because, indeed, we see that there is not that analogy between discords as between things that are completely opposite."

Harmony can come from dissimilar sounds, but no such harmony can come from the self-loving courtiers because they are so similar in their Self-Love.

Making these self-loving courtiers harmonize is a labor worthy of Hercules, who performed twelve nearly impossible-to-accomplish labors.

Arete, who wanted the vain courtiers to participate in Cynthia's revels, said:

"There is your error. For Hermes' wand charms the disorders of tumultuous ghosts — one of Mercury's responsibilities is to lead the ghosts of the dead to the Underworld — and the strife of Chaos then did cease when better light than Nature's did arrive.

"Just like those two examples, what could never in itself agree forgets the eccentric property and turns forthwith regular at the sight of her whose scepter guides the flowing ocean."

In Ptolemaic astronomy, an eccentric orbit is one whose exact center is not the Earth.

Cynthia is goddess of the Moon, and she has power over the tides. Queen Elizabeth I, whom Cynthia often represents in poetry written during Elizabeth's reign, had much sea power.

Just the sight of Cynthia ought to turn the vain courtiers away from their vanity and toward Proper Pride.

Arete continued:

"And even if the sight of Cynthia does not work its transformative magic on the self-loving courtiers, yet respect of majesty, the place, and the presence of Cynthia will keep most of them, being either courtiers or not wholly rude, within ring — within limits.

"This is true especially when they are not presented as themselves, but are masked like others. For, in truth, not so to incorporate them — that is, make them into a team, or make them a new body — could be nothing else than 1) like a state ungoverned, without laws, or 2) a body made of nothing but diseases.

"The one state would be through impotency poor and wretched.

"The other state would be, because of the anarchy, absurd."

Criticus next argued that people other than the vain courtiers ought to participate in Cynthia's revels:

"But lady, for the revelers themselves it would be better, in my poor conceit — understanding and opinion — that others would be employed to participate in the revels; for such as are unfit to be in Cynthia's court can seem no less unfit to be in Cynthia's entertainments."

Arete then argued that Cynthia had a particular purpose for holding her revels, and that purpose was to create a reformation:

"That is not done, my Criticus, without particular knowledge of the goddess' mind.

"Cynthia, who holds true intelligence and information about what follies have crept into her palace, has resolved on holding entertainments and triumphs; under that pretext, she has resolved to have them muster in their pomp and fullness, so that she might more strictly and to the root effect the reformation she intends."

Convinced by Arete's words, Criticus agreed to do what Arete and Cynthia wished him to do:

"I now conceive Cynthia's heavenly drift in all, and I will apply my spirits to serve thy will.

"Oh, thou, you are the very power by which I am, and but for which it would be in vain to be.

"You are chief and are second only to Diana.

"You are virgin, heavenly fair, admired Arete, admired by them whose souls are not enkindled — set on fire with lust — by the senses …

"Disdain not my chaste fire, but feed the flame

"Devoted truly to thy gracious name!"

Arete replied:

"Leave — cease — to suspect us. Criticus shall find

"As we are now most dear, we'll prove most kind."

A voice from another room called, "Arete!"

Arete said, "Listen, I am called."

She exited.

Alone, Criticus said to himself:

"I will follow instantly."

He then began a prayer to Apollo and Mercury:

"Phoebus Apollo, if with ancient rites and due devotions, I have ever hung elaborate paeans on thy golden shrine or sung thy triumphs in a lofty strain, fit for a theater of gods to hear, and thou the other son of mighty Jove, Cyllenian Mercury — who was born on Mount Cellene to his mother, Maia — sweet Maia's joy …"

He then asked for something good:

"… if in the busy tumults of the mind thou ever have illuminated my path, for which thine altars I have often perfumed and decked thy statue with many-colored flowers:

"Now cause invention to thrive in this glorious court,

"So that not of bounty only, but of right,

"Cynthia may grace and give it life by sight!"

Just the sight of Cynthia will grace the court and give it sight.

Just seeing Cynthia will improve the vain courtiers and make them better.

CHAPTER 5

— 5.1 —

Hesperus, Cynthia, Arete, Timè, Phronesis, and Thauma were together.

Hesperus is the personification of the evening star.

The name "Timè" means "Honor."

The name "Phronesis" means "Prudence."

The name "Thauma" means "Wonder."

Hesperus sang a hymn to Cynthia, who was both a Moon goddess and the goddess of hunting:

"Queen and huntress, chaste and fair,

"Now the Sun is laid to sleep,

"Seated in thy silver chair,

"State in wonted [accustomed] manner keep;"

"To keep state" means "to maintain one's dignity" and "to observe the ceremony that a person of high rank deserves."

Hesperus continued singing:

"Hesperus entreats thy light,

"Goddess excellently bright.

"Earth, let not thy envious [malicious] shade

"Dare itself to interpose!"

In other words: Earth, don't cause a lunar eclipse.

Hesperus continued singing:

"Cynthia's shining orb [the Moon] was made

"Heaven to clear, when day did close.

"Bless us then with wished [wished-for] sight,

"Goddess excellently bright.

"Lay thy bow of pearl apart,

"And thy crystal-shining quiver;

"Give unto the flying hart [fleeing deer, fleeing heart]

"Space to breathe, how short soever [however short];"

In other words: Be merciful to the deer who flee from you in your character as a huntress and be merciful to the hearts of the vain courtiers who flee from correct behavior.

Hesperus continued singing:

"*Thou, that mak'st [who make] a day of night,*

"*Goddess excellently bright!*"

A bright Moon reflects light by which we can see at night.

Hesperus exited.

Cynthia/Diana began to speak.

First, she denied that she is like a malicious miser:

"When has Diana, like an envious wretch who glitters and is splendid only to his soothed — comforted and flattered — self, denying to the world the precious use of hoarded wealth, withheld her friendly aid?"

She is not a miser because she gives light to people on Earth:

"Monthly we expend our constantly repaired — waning and waxing — shine, and we do not forbid our virgin-waxen torch to burn and blaze while nutriment does last.

"Our virgin-waxen torch, once consumed, out of Jove's treasury anew we take, and stick it in our sphere to give the mutinous race of lacking men their looked-for light."

She then asked if the receivers of her — the Moon's — light deserve to receive it:

"Yet what is their desert? Do they deserve the light?

"Bounty is wronged, interpreted as due.

"Mortals can challenge not a ray by right,

"Yet they do expect the whole of Cynthia's light.

"But if deities were to withdraw their gifts because of human follies, what would men deserve but death and darkness?"

According to Cynthia, she and other high beings ought to do things worthily for their own sakes — simply because the things are worthy and because the high beings are worthy:

"It behooves the high beings for their own sakes to do things worthily."

Arete said:

"What you said is most true, most sacred goddess, for the heavens receive no good from all the good they do.

"Neither Jove, nor you, nor other heavenly powers are fed with fumes which rise from incense, or sacrifices reeking — steaming — in their bloody gore."

When the ancient Greeks sacrificed, they ate the meat, and the smoke from the sacrificial fires rose to Mount Olympus.

Arete continued:

"Yet because of the care and concern that you have for mortals, whose proper good it is that they be so, you well are pleased with odors redolent."

The gods are happy with the odor of roasting meat from the sacrificial fires. This shows their concern for human beings, whom they allow to eat the meat.

Arete continued:

"But ignorant is all the race of men,

"Which always complains, not knowing why or when."

According to Arete, human beings always complain about the gods although they ought not to.

Cynthia said:

"Else, noble Arete, they would not blame and tax, either as unjust or as proud, thy Cynthia in the things that are indeed the greatest glories in our starry crown.

"Such a great glory is our chastity, which safely scorns not love — for who more fervently loves immortal honor and divine renown?

"Instead, our chastity scorns giddy Cupid, Venus' frantic son.

"Yet, Arete, neither night nor court would enjoy our light, if by this veiled and dimmed light, we just discerned — what we in fact do not discern — even the least of imputations standing ready to sprinkle our unspotted reputation with note of lightness — unchastity — from these imminent revels.

"If we did discern such imputations, not even for the empire and rulership of the universe would either night or court enjoy any shine or grace at all of ours.

"Let me repeat:

"If we did discern such imputations, neither night nor court would unhappily — inappropriately — enjoy any shine or grace at all of ours."

She continued:

"Place and occasion are two privy thieves, and from poor innocent ladies often steal the best of things: an honorable name.

"To stay with follies, or where faults may be,

"Infers a crime, although the party be free."

She meant "be free of crime."

The word "crime" means "sin."

Arete said:

"How Cynthianly — that is, how worthily and like herself — the matchless Cynthia speaks!

"Infinite jealousies, infinite watchfulness, do watch about the true virginity, but Phoebe [Cynthia as Moon goddess] lives free from all not only fault, but as from thought, so from suspicion free."

This kind of jealousy is devotion and eagerness to serve.

Arete continued:

"Thy presence broad-seals — gives the highest authorization to — our delights for pure.

"What's done in Cynthia's sight is done safely and securely."

Cynthia said:

"That, then, so answered, dearest Arete, what the argument — subject and theme — or of what sort our entertainments are likely to be this night, I will not demand to know.

"Nothing that duty and desire to please bears written in the forehead — plainly expressed — comes amiss.

"But unto whose invention must we owe the complement — completion — of this night's entertainment? Who is the author?"

Arete said:

"Excellent goddess, the credit for the entertainment is due to a man's inventiveness, whose worth, without hyperbole, I thus may praise:

"He is one, at least, who is studious of deserving well, and, to speak the truth, indeed he is deserving well.

"Potential merit stands for actual where only opportunity is missing.

"Neither will nor power are missing in him: Both of them in him abound.

"He is one whom the Muses and Minerva love — for whom should they love more than Criticus, whom Phoebus the god of poetry, although not Lady Fortune, holds dear?

"And, which argues convincingly excellence in him, he is a principal admirer of yourself.

"Even through the ungentle injuries of fate, and difficulties, which choke virtue, thus much of him appears.

"What other things of farther note do lie unborn in him, them I leave for nourishing cherishing to show, and for a goddess graciously to judge."

Cynthia said:

"We have already judged him, Arete.

"Nor are we ignorant how noble minds suffer too much through those indignities that times and vicious persons cast on them.

"Ourself have always vowed to esteem virtue as worthy in itself, and so esteem fortune as base.

"Virtue is first in worth, and so virtue is first in place.

"Nor farther notice, Arete, we crave than thine approval's sovereign warranty.

"Let it be thy care to make us known to him.

"Cynthia shall brighten what the world made dim."

— 5.2 —

The First Masque began.

Cupid, appearing like Anteros, held a crystal globe, aka crystal ball.

Anteros is Anti-Eros, the half-brother and enemy to Eros, who is also known as Cupid. Ben Jonson regarded Anti-Eros highly as the god of Requited Love and as Love of Virtue. Cupid, in contrast, is often a causer of chaos.

In his costume as Anteros, Cupid carried a bow and arrows.

Appearing but not speaking in the masque were these four allegorical characters:

Philautia appeared as Storge, or Natural Affection. Her motto is "Each to his own standard."

Gelaia appeared as Aglaia, or Pleasant and Delectable Conversation. Her motto is "I dispel the clouds of worry."

Phantaste appeared as Euphantaste, or Wittiness. Her motto is "Thus the praise of wit [increases]."

Moria appeared as Apheleia, or Simplicity. Her motto is "No makeup is present."

The masquers carried imprese with mottoes. These imprese were pasteboard shields bearing a symbolic picture called a device. Each shield also bore a motto.

The four female allegorical characters served their queen, **Perfection**.

Cupid, in the character of Anteros, said:

"Clear pearl of heaven, and not to be farther ambitious in titles, Cynthia:

"The fame of this illustrious night, among others, has also drawn these four fair virgins from the palace of their queen, **Perfection** — a word that makes no sufficient difference between hers and thine — to visit thy imperial court; for she, their sovereign lady, not finding where to dwell among men, before her return to heaven, advised them wholly to consecrate themselves to thy celestial service, as in Cynthia's clear spirit — the proper element and sphere of virtues — they should behold not her alone, their ever honored mistress, but themselves, more truly themselves, to live enthroned.

"**Perfection** herself would have commended them unto thy favor more particularly, except that she knows no commendation is more available with thee than that of proper virtue.

"Nevertheless, she willed them to present this crystal globe, a note of monarchy and symbol of perfection, to thy more worthy deity; which as here by me they most humbly do, so among the rarities thereof, that is the chief, to show whatsoever the world has excellent, howsoever remote and various.

"But your irradiate — illuminate — judgment will soon look into the crystal ball and discover the secrets of this little crystal world.

"The four virgins themselves, to appear the more plainly, because they know nothing more odious than false pretexts, have chosen to express their several qualities thus in several colors.

1. Natural Affection. Allowable Self-Love.

"The first, in citron — pale yellow — color, is **Natural Affection**, which given to us to procure our good, is sometimes called Storge, and as everyone is nearest to himself, so this handmaid of Reason, **Allowable Self-Love**, as it is without harm, so are none without it; her place in the court of Perfection was to quicken minds in the pursuit of honor.

"Her device is a perpendicular level upon a cube or square."

These items are used in making measurements.

Cupid, in the character of Anteros, continued:

"The motto is *se suo modulo* [each to his own standard], alluding to that true measure of one's self, which as everyone ought to make, so is it most conspicuous in thy divine example."

Aristotle in his *Nicomachian Ethics* made a distinction between Vicious Self-Love and Virtuous Self-Love. A person who has Virtuous Self-Love will love and respect him- or herself and will want to preserve that self. Such a person will have Proper Pride.

Horace in his *Epistles* 1.7.9 wrote "*metiri se quemque suo modulo ac pede verum est.*" Translation: "Every man should measure himself by his own standard and yardstick."

2. Delectable and Pleasant Conversation.

"The second, in green, is Aglaia, **Delectable and Pleasant Conversation**, whose property it is to move a kindly delight, and sometimes not without laughter.

"Her office is to entertain assemblies and to keep societies together with fair familiarity.

"Her device is this: within a ring of clouds, a heart with shine about it.

"The motto *curarum nubila pello* [I dispel the clouds of worry] is an allegory of Cynthia's light, which no less clears the sky than her fair mirth clears the heart.

3. Wittiness.

"The third, in a pale mantle spangled all over, is Euphantaste, a well-conceited **Wittiness**, and employed in honoring the court with the riches of her pure invention.

"Her device is a crescent upon a petasus, aka a mercurial (worn, with additional wings, by Mercury) hat with a low crown and broad brim.

"Her motto, *sic laus ingenii* [thus the praise of wit], infers that the praise and glory of wit does ever increase as does thy growing Moon.

4. Simplicity.

"The fourth, in white, is Apheleia, a nymph as pure and simple as the soul, or as an abrase table [a blank tablet], and is therefore called **Simplicity**; without folds, aka without pleats in which items can be hidden, without color, without counterfeit, and, to speak plainly, plainness itself. Her device is no device.

"The motto under her silver shield is *omnis abest fucus* [no makeup is present], alluding to thy spotless self, who are as far from impurity as from mortality."

Anteros. Anti-Eros.

Cupid, in the character of Anteros, then identified whom he was portraying:

"I myself, celestial goddess, more fit for the court of Cynthia than the arbors of Cythere, am called Anteros, or **Love's Enemy**; the more welcome therefore to thy court and the fitter to conduct this *quaternion* [set of four], who as they are thy professed votaries, and for that cause adversaries to Love, yet thee, perpetual virgin, they both love and vow to love eternally."

Various kinds of Love exist, not all of them good.

Cynthia values Love of Virtue. She does not value the kind of Love that is Lust.

Cythere, aka Cythera, is the name of the island where Venus was born.

Cynthia looked into the crystal ball and saw a vision of Queen Elizabeth:

"Not without wonder, nor without delight, my eyes have viewed in contemplation's depth — the depth of this crystal ball — this work of wit divine and excellent.

"What shape, what substance, or what unknown power, in virgin's clothing crowned with the laurel leaves of victory and the olive branches of peace woven in between, on sea-girt rock shines similar to a goddess?

"O front [forehead]! O face! O all celestial sure and more than mortal!

"Arete, behold another Cynthia, and another queen, whose glory, like a lasting plenilune — full Moon — seems ignorant of what it is to wane.

"Not under heaven could an object be found more fit to please."

Cynthia then called for Criticus:

"Let Criticus approach.

"Bounty forbids to pall and make pale our thanks with delay, or to defer our favor after view.

"The time of grace is, when the cause is new."

Criticus entered the scene.

Arete said:

"Look, here is the man, celestial Delia, who, like a circle bounded in itself, contains as much as man in fullness may.

"Look, here is the man, who, not of usual earth, but of that nobler and more precious mold — Earth — which Phoebus' self does temper, is composed.

"And who, even if all were not rewarding him, yet to himself he would not be lacking. He would have what he needs.

"The gain of thy favor is his greatest and best ambition,

"And the best goal of his labor; he is a man who, humble in his height,

"Stands fixed silent in thy glorious sight."

Cynthia said:

"With no less pleasure than we have beheld this precious crystal, a work of rarest wit, our eye does read thee, now, our Criticus, whom learning, virtue, and lastly our favor, exempts from the gloomy multitude.

"With common eye the supreme — the highest — should not see.

"Henceforth be ours, the more thyself to be."

Criticus replied:

"Heaven's purest light, whose orb may be eclipsed, but not thy praise, divinest Cynthia, how much too narrow for so high a grace thy, save therein, unworthy Criticus finds himself!

"May thy fame and thine honors shine forever, as thy beauties do.

"In me they must shine; they are my dark world's chiefest lights, by whose propitious beams my powers are raised to hope some part of those most lofty points that blessed Arete has pleased to name as landmarks to which my endeavor's steps should bend.

"Mine, as begun at thee, in thee must end."

The Second Masque began.

Mercury appeared as a page.

Appearing but not speaking in the masque were these people, who were playing allegorical characters:

Amorphus appeared as Eucosmos. The name means "Orderly" and "Well-Mannered."

Hedon appeared as Euphathes. The name means "Enjoying Good Things."

Anaides appeared as Eutolmos. The name means "Brave-Spirited."

Asotus appeared as Eucolos. The name means "Good-Natured" and "Benevolent."

They were outfitted with suitable heraldic devices, including javelins.

They were the sons of **Eutaxia**. The name means **Orderly Behavior**: Eutaxia is **Orderly Behaved and Well-Mannered**.

Mercury, in the character of a page, greeted Cynthia:

"Sister of Phoebus Apollo, to whose bright orb we owe that which we do not complain of his absence."

Apollo's bright orb is the Sun, but the bright orb here is the brightly lit Moon, because of whose brightness no one needed to complain about the absence of the Sun. Of course, the Moon does not produce its own light — it instead reflects the light of the Sun.

Mercury, in the character of a page, presented the four allegorical beings:

"These four brethren — for they are brethren and sons of Eutaxia, aka **Orderly Behavior**, a lady known and highly beloved of your resplendent deity, and these brethren are not able to be absent when Cynthia holds a ceremonial event — dutifully move themselves into thy presence; for, as there are four cardinal virtues upon which the whole frame of the court does move, so are these the four cardinal properties without which the body of compliment does not move."

The four cardinal virtues are Justice, Prudence, Temperance, and Fortitude.

Mercury, in the character of a page, continued:

"With these four silver javelins, ceremonial weapons that they bear in their hands, they support in princes' courts the stateliness of the presence chamber, as by office they are obliged; which though here they may seem superfluous, yet for honor's sake they thus presume to visit thee, having also been employed in the palace of Queen Perfection.

"And though to them, who would make themselves gracious to a goddess, sacrifices would be fitter than presents or imprese, yet they both hope thy favor, and, in place of either, use several symbols containing the titles of thy imperial dignity.

1. Eucosmos: Neat and Elegant.

"The hithermost, in the robe with the blue and green contrasting and changeable color effects, is the commendably fashionable gallant, **Eucosmos**. His courtly outfit is the grace of the presence and delight of the surveying eye; he is the gallant whom ladies understand by the names of **Neat and Elegant**. His symbol is *divae virgini* [to the divine virgin] in which he would express thy deity's principal glory, which has always been virginity.

2. Eupathes: Enjoying Good Things.

"The second, in the rich accoutrement and robe of purple impaled — bisected — with a vertical line of gold, is **Eupathes**, who entertains his mind with a harmless but not careless variety. All the objects of his senses are sumptuous. He is a gallant who without excess can make use of superfluities, go richly in embroideries, jewels, and what not, without vanity, and dine delicately without gluttony. And therefore, not without cause, he is universally thought to be of fine humor. His symbol is *divae optimae* [to the best goddess], an attribute to express thy goodness in which thou so resemble Jove, thy father.

3. Eutolmos: Brave-Spirited; Good Audacity.

"The third, in the blush-colored suit, is **Eutolmos**, as duly respecting others as never neglecting himself. He is commonly known by the title of **Good Audacity**; he is a guest most acceptable at courts and courtly assemblies. His symbol is *divae viragini* [to the divine virago, aka female warrior], to express thy hardy courage in chase of savage beasts that harbor in woods and wilderness."

Cynthia is a huntress.

4. Eucolos: Good-Natured, Kind, and Benevolent; Truly Beneficent.

"The fourth, in watchet-tinsel [sky-blue cloth with gold or silver thread], is the **kind and truly beneficent Eucolos**, who imparts not without respect, but yet without difficulty, and has the happiness to make every kindness seem double, by the timely and freely bestowing thereof."

A proverb stated that the person who gives quickly gives twice.

"He is the chief of them who, by the common people, are said to be of good nature. His symbol is *divae maximae* [to the best goddess], an additional name to signify thy greatness, which in Heaven, Earth, and Hell is formidable."

Cynthia is a tripartite goddess: a goddess with three forms.

In Heaven, she is Luna, goddess of the Moon.

On Earth, she is Diana, goddess of the hunt.

In Hell, she is Hecate, goddess of witchcraft.

— 5.5 —

The two masques joined: a masque of four women and a masque of four men. Because they were wearing masks, their identities were not readily apparent to Cupid.

Cupid asked Mercury, "Isn't that Amorphus, the traveler?"

Mercury replied, "As though it could be anyone else. Don't you see how his legs are in travail with a measure?"

"Hedon, thy master, is next," Cupid said.

"What, will Cupid turn nomenclator — announcer — and cry out the names?" Mercury asked.

"No, indeed, but I have a comedy in mind that would not be lost for a kingdom," Cupid said.

Cupid has the power — usually — to make the four women and the four men fall in love. Often, the result of falling in love is comedy.

"In good time, for Cupid will prove the comedy," Mercury said.

One way to interpret this sentence is that Cupid will be the one who is laughed at.

"Mercury, I am studying how to be a matchmaker and match them," Cupid said.

"How to mismatch them would be harder," Mercury replied.

They were all full of Self-Love, and so they were all similar.

"It is the nymphs who must do it," Cupid said. "I shall entertain myself with their passions above measure — exceedingly."

"Those nymphs need to be tamed a little indeed, but I fear thou have not the arrows necessary for the purpose," Mercury said.

"Oh, yes, I do," Cupid said. "Here are arrows of all sorts: flights, rovers, and butt-shafts."

Because he was impersonating Anteros, Cupid had a bow and arrows.

Flights are light arrows that can travel a long distance. Rovers are arrows for shooting at various targets selected by the archer. Butt-shafts are blunt arrows.

Cupid added, "But I can wound with a brandish — just by shaking an arrow at someone — and never draw bow for the matter."

144

"I cannot but believe it, my invisible archer, and yet I think you are wearisome," Mercury said.

As gods, Mercury and Cupid can turn themselves invisible.

Gods can definitely get on each other's nerves.

Cupid said:

"It behooves me to be somewhat circumspect, Mercury, for if Cynthia should hear the twang of my bow, she'll come close to whipping me with the string.

"Therefore, to prevent that, I thus discharge a brandish upon — it makes no matter which of the couples.

"Phantaste and Amorphus, I brandish my arrow at you."

If all were to go as Cupid expected, Phantaste and Amorphus would now fall in love.

Mercury asked, "Will the shaking of a shaft strike them into such a fever of affection?"

"As well as the wink of an eye," Cupid said. "But I pray thee hinder me not with thy prattle."

"Jove forbid I hinder thee!" Mercury said. "By the Virgin Mary, all that I fear is Cynthia's presence, which, with the cold of her chastity, casts such an antiperistasis — contrary circumstance — about the place that no heat of thine will tarry with the patient."

The coldness of Cynthia's chastity may make it impossible for Cupid's arrows to cause sexual heat in anyone at whom he brandishes his arrow.

Cupid said, "It will tarry the rather, for the antiperistasis will keep it in."

Cupid thought that Cynthia's chastity would serve as an outer boundary that would keep sexual heat inside Phantaste and Amorphus. Think of an igloo with a fire inside.

"I long to see the experiment," Mercury said.

"Why, their bone marrow boils already, or else they have all been turned into eunuchs," Cupid said.

Phantaste and Amorphus should already be deeply in love.

"Nay, if it is so, I'll give over speaking, and be a spectator only," Mercury said.

All danced to the first strain of music.

Full of Self-Love, Amorphus said to himself, "Cynthia, by my bright soul, is a completely exquisite and splendidious and magnificent lady, yet Amorphus, I think, has seen more fashions, and I am sure I have seen more countries. But whether I have or not, what need have we to gaze on Cynthia when we have ourself to admire?"

Full of Self-Love, Phantaste said to herself, "Oh, excellent Cynthia! Yet if Phantaste sat where she does and had such a tire — a headdress — on her head (for attire can do much) ... I say no more — but goddesses are goddesses, and Phantaste is as she is! I wish the revels were done at once, so I might go to my school of glass — my mirror — again and learn to do myself right after all this ruffling."

"Ruffling" means "contending." The Self-Lovers were contending with Cynthia for supremacy.

Amorphus loved himself, and Phantaste loved herself. They doted on themselves, not on each other. They loved themselves more than they loved Cynthia.

Phantaste wanted to work on her makeup to make it better.

Mercury said sarcastically, "How are things now, Cupid? Here's a wonderful change as a result of your brandishing your arrows! Don't you hear how they dote?"

"What prodigy is this?" Cupid said. "No word of love? No mention of love? No motion toward each other? No commotion?"

"Not a word, my little hell-fire, not a word," Mercury said.

Cupid's arrows inflame the heart, and so he can be called a little hell-fire.

"Are my darts enchanted?" Cupid said. "Is their vigor gone? Is their virtue —"

Mercury said, "What? Cupid turned jealous of himself? Cupid troubled that his power has gone? Ha, ha, ha!"

"Does Mercury laugh?" Cupid asked.

"Is Cupid angry?" Mercury asked.

"Hasn't he reason to be angry, when his purpose is so laughed at?" Cupid asked.

His purpose was to cause comedy by having Phantaste and Amorphus fall in love. Mercury was laughing because Cupid could not accomplish his purpose.

"A splendid comedy; it shall be titled Cupid's Comedy," Mercury said.

"Do not scorn us, Hermes," Cupid said.

Mercury/Hermes replied, "Choler, aka Anger, and Cupid are two fiery things; I do not scorn them. But I see that come to pass which I presaged in the beginning."

Earlier, Mercury had said, "By the Virgin Mary, all that I fear is Cynthia's presence, which, with the cold of her chastity, casts such an antiperistasis — contrary circumstance — about the place that no heat of thine will tarry with the patient."

In other words, he had worried that Cupid's arrows would have no effect so near Cynthia.

"You cannot tell," Cupid said. "Perhaps the medicine will not work as soon upon some as upon others. It may be the rest are not so resty — so sluggish."

Mercury said, "*Ex ungue*. You know the old adage: As these, so are the remainder."

Ex ungue leonum is a proverb: "From the claw of a lion," you may discover its size.

If Cupid's arrows didn't work on Phantaste and Amorphus, chances were excellent that they would not work on other couples.

Cupid said, "I'll try again. This is the same shaft with which I wounded Argurion."

Argurion had fallen in love with Asotus after Cupid had brandished one of his arrows at her.

"Aye, but let me save you a labor, Cupid," Mercury said. "There were certain bottles of water fetched and drunk off, since that time, by these gallants."

"May Jove strike me into Earth!" Cupid said. "The Fountain of Self-Love!"

A person who is excessively in love with him- or herself may find it difficult or impossible to fall in love with someone else.

"Don't faint, Cupid," Mercury said.

"I did not remember that," Cupid said.

Mercury said:

"Indeed, it was ominous to take the name of Anteros upon you; you don't know what charm or enchantment lies in the word.

"You saw I did not dare to venture upon any device or plot in our presentation, but instead I was content to be no other than a simple page.

"Your arrows' properties, to keep decorum and appropriateness, Cupid, are suited, it would seem, to the nature of him whom you impersonate: Anteros."

Cupid's arrows could not now be used to create romantic drama.

"This is an indignity not to be borne!" Cupid said.

"Nay, rather it is an attempt to have been forborne," Mercury said. "You ought not to have attempted to use your arrows to make them fall in love."

Cupid said to himself:

"How might I revenge myself on this insulting Mercury?

"There's Criticus, his minion; he has not tasted of this water. It shall be so."

All danced to the second strain of music.

Cupid asked Mercury, "Has Criticus turned dotard on himself, too? Is he in love with himself, too?"

Mercury answered, "That does not follow from the fact that the venom of your shafts cannot pierce him."

The venom of Cupid's arrows could not pierce Criticus, but it does not follow that Criticus was filled with Self-Love.

"As though there were one antidote for these, and another for him?" Cupid asked.

The antidote for the foolish courtiers was their Self-Love. The antidote for Criticus was his strength of character and the protection of Cynthia.

"As though there were not two antidotes!" Mercury said. "Or as if one effect might not arise from diverse causes? What do you say to Cynthia, Arete, Phronesis, Timè, and others there?"

These beings were all immune to Cupid's arrows.

"They are divine," Cupid answered.

"And Criticus aspires to be so," Mercury said.

Criticus aspired to the highest values and behavior.

"But that shall not serve him," Cupid said. "That shall not be of use to him when I use my powers on him."

"It is likely to serve him prettily well at this time," Mercury said. "But Cupid has grown too covetous because he will not spare one of a multitude."

In Genesis 18:23-33, Abraham bargains with God not to destroy Sodom if 50 righteous people are found to reside there. Abraham then bargains the number down to 45, then 40, 30, 20, and finally 10. Eventually, one righteous man — Lot — is found. God destroys Sodom, but Lot and his family flee from the destruction.

"One is more than a multitude," Cupid said.

One virtuous man is worth more than a multitude of fools.

Not sparing one virtuous man is more destructive than not sparing a multitude of fools.

Mercury said, "Arete's favor makes anyone shot-proof against thee, Cupid."

All danced to the third strain of music.

Mercury then said, "Please, light honey-bee, remember thou are not now in Adonis' garden, but in Cynthia's presence, where thorns lie in garrison about the roses."

Adonis was a mortal lover of Venus.

Mercury then said, "Quiet, Cynthia speaks."

Cynthia now began to speak to the ladies and gallants. In doing so, she was speaking to the Virtues whom the foolish courtiers filled with Self-Love were portraying. She was not speaking to the foolish courtiers who were portraying those virtues.

Using the third person and the regal plural, and sometimes calling herself "Diana," Cynthia said:

"Ladies and gallants,

"To give a timely period — end — to our entertainments, let us conclude them with declining night; dawn is coming soon. Our empire is only the darker half of the 24-hour day.

"If you judge to have earned Diana's thanks to be any recompense for your fair pains, Diana grants to you her thanks, and bestows their crown to gratify your acceptable zeal.

"For you are not those who, as some have done, censure and judge us as too severe and sour.

"Instead, you judge us, as, more rightly, gracious to the good.

"Although we do not deny that unto the proud or the profane, we are perhaps indeed austere:

"For so Actaeon, by presuming far, did, to our grief, incur a fatal doom, and so swollen-with-pride Niobe, comparing more than he (Actaeon) presumed, was trophied into stone."

Niobe compared herself to Leto, Cynthia's mother, and she said that she was more worthy of admiration than Leto because Leto had given birth to only one son and only one daughter, while Niobe had given birth to six sons and six daughters. As punishment for her egotistic comparison, Niobe was transformed into a stone trophy. Ancient Roman generals could make a trophy by displaying an enemy general's armor on a tree trunk whose branches had been lopped off: This would be a monument to commemorate a victory.

Actaeon was out hunting, and he saw Cynthia, a virgin goddess, bathing naked. As punishment for his presumption and impure thoughts, Cynthia punished him by turning him into a stag. Actaeon's own hounds killed him.

Cynthia continued:

"But are we therefore judged to be too extreme?

"Does it seem to be no crime to enter sacred bowers and to pollute hallowed places most lewdly with impure gaze?"

Actaeon did that.

Cynthia continued:

"Does it seem to be no crime to brave and defy a deity?"

Niobe did that.

Cynthia continued:

"Let mortals learn to make religion of 'offending' heaven, and not at all to censure powers divine.

"To men, this argument should stand for firm:

"A goddess did it; therefore, it was good."

Even when heaven offends or seems to offend, mortals ought not to judge it.

Cynthia continued:

"We are not cruel, nor do we delight in blood.

"But what have these serious repetitions of already-known narratives about Actaeon and Niobe to do with revels and the entertainments of court?

"We do not intend to sour your late delights with harsh expostulation. Let it suffice that we take notice of and can take revenge on these calumnious and lewd blasphemies.

"For we are no less Cynthia than we were, nor is our power, other than as ourself, the same, although we have now put on no tire of shine — shiny headdress — except that which mortal eyes undazzled may endure."

Mortal eyes can endure looking at the Moon, but they are blinded when looking at the Sun. Cynthia is careful not to overwhelm mortals with her shine. Doing so can destroy them.

Jupiter, king of the gods, promised to give Semele, a mortal woman, anything she wanted if she would sleep with him. After they had slept together, she told him that she wanted to see him in his full divine glory rather than in just the form he took when he appeared to mortals. Because he had sworn an inviolable oath, he did as she requested. Unable to endure the sight, she burst into flames.

Cynthia continued:

"Years are beneath the spheres, and time makes weak the things under heaven; time does not make weak the powers which govern heaven."

The first Ptolemaic sphere around the Earth was that of the Moon. According to Ptolemy, crystalline spheres have embedded in them the planets and the stars.

Cynthia continued:

"And although ourself be in ourself secure, yet let mortals not claim as a right for themselves immunity from ourself.

"Lo, this is all:

"Honor has store of spleen, but lacks gall."

In other words: Honor is quick to become angry, but Honor does not carry around bitterness after becoming angry.

Mankind cannot expect to be immune from Cynthia's anger; she does grow angry at calumnious and lewd blasphemies.

Cynthia continued:

"Once more, we cast the slumber of our thanks on your taken toil, which here let take an end."

She was bringing their toil (of performing the masque) to an end. The slumber of her thanks is to allow them to rest.

Cynthia continued:

"And so that we do not mistake your several worths, nor you our favor, from yourselves remove what makes you not yourselves, those clouds of mask.

"Particular pains, particular thanks do ask."

The eight foolish courtiers — four men and four women — took off their masks, revealing their real identities.

Cynthia said:

"Are we contemned and scorned?

"Is there so little awe of our disdain that any, under trust of their disguise, would mix themselves with others of the court?

"And, without forehead — shame — boldly press so far that nowhere farther is left that they can invade?

"How apt is lenity to be abused? Severity to be loathed?

"And yet, how much more does the seeming face of neighbor virtues, and their borrowed names, add of lewd boldness to loose vanities!

"Who would have thought that Philautia did dare either to have usurped noble Storge's name and with that theft to have dared to approach our eyes?

"Who would have thought that all of them should hope so much of our connivance — tacit approval — as to come to grace themselves with titles not their own?

"Instead of medicines, have we maladies?

"And such impostumes — moral abscesses — as Phantaste is do grow in our palace? We must lance these sores, or all will putrefy."

Abscessed sores are pierced with a lancet so that the pus can drain out and the sore can heal.

Cynthia continued:

"Nor are these all, for we suspect a farther fraud than this.

"Take off our veil so that shadows may depart and shapes appear, beloved Arete."

Arete took the veil from Cynthia's face.

The entire presence chamber brightened.

Cynthia said:

"So.

"Another face of things presents itself than did recently.

"What, feathered Cupid masked, and masked to appear like Anteros?

"But even more strange! Dear Mercury, our half-brother, like a page, to countenance and support the ambush of the boy?"

Cynthia and Mercury share the same father: Jupiter.

Cupid had planned to play tricks in Cynthia's presence chamber. Mercury had not revealed Cupid's plot to Cynthia, and so he had tacitly approved of it.

Cynthia continued:

"Nor ends our discovery as yet.

"Gelaia is now like a nymph, who just a while ago in male attire did serve Anaides as a page?

"Cupid came here to find entertainment and game. He, heretofore, has been too conversant among our train of servants, but he has never felt revenge.

"And Mercury gave Cupid company.

"Cupid, we must confess this time of mirth, which was proclaimed by us, gave opportunity to thy attempts to play tricks, although no privilege.

"Tempt us no farther, we cannot endure thy presence longer; vanish, go away from here. Go away!"

Cupid exited.

Cynthia continued:

"You, Mercury, we must entreat to stay, and hear what we determine of the rest, for in this plot you have the deepest hand.

"But — because we do not mean a censorian — too severe — task and yet we do mean to lance these ulcers grown so ripe and so ready to be lanced — dear Arete and Criticus, to you we give the charge and responsibility of inflicting punishment.

"Impose what pains you please. The incurable cut off, the rest reform.

"Remember always what we first decreed,

"Since revels were proclaimed, let now none bleed."

Cynthia wanted Arete and Criticus to decide what will be the punishment, but the punishment may not be death.

Arete said:

"How well Diana can distinguish times and sort her censures! Keeping to herself the doom — the judgment — of gods, leaving the rest to us!

"Come, cite them — summon them to court — Criticus, and then proceed."

Criticus summoned the female offenders:

"First Philautia, for she was the first,

"Then light [trivial] Gelaia in Aglaia's name,

"Thirdly Phantaste, and Moria next,

"You are all strong follies, and of the female company."

Criticus then summoned the male offenders:

"Amorphus, or Eucosmos counterfeit,

"Voluptuous [lustful] Hedon taken for Eupathes,

"Shameless Anaides, and Asotus last,

"With his two pages, Morus and Prosaites;

"And thou, the traveler's evil, Cos, approach,

"All of you are impostors, and male deformities."

The travelers' evil is lying. Many travelers made up fantastic stories about their travels.

Self-Love, aka Pride, is the foundation of the other Seven Deadly Sins.

Arete said to Criticus:

"Go forward and continue, for I delegate my power, and I decree that at thy mercy they do stand — the mercy of you whom they so often so plainly scorned before.

"It is virtue that they lack, and lacking it,

"Honor no garment to their backs can fit."

"Now, Criticus, use your discretion."

Criticus, who was obliged to be both severe and merciful, said:

"Adored Cynthia, and bright Arete, another might seem fitter for this task than I, Criticus, except that you do not judge that to be so.

"For I, not to appear vindictive and revengeful, or mindful of contempts and insults, which I condemned and scorned as done out of impotence, must be negligent of my duty.

"As I was the author in some sort of this masque in order to bring knowledge of them into Cynthia's sight, I should be much severer to revenge the indignity hence issuing to her name.

"But there's not one of these who are unpained, or by themselves unpunished; for vice is like a fury and a Fury to the vicious mind, and it turns delight itself into punishment.

"But we must go forward and continue to define their doom."

He said to the foolish courtiers (including the foolish ladies of the court) and foolish pages:

"You are offenders, and that you must confess.

"Do you confess it?"

All the foolish courtiers and foolish pages said, "We do."

Criticus then asked:

"And do you acknowledge that you deserve sharp correction?"

All the foolish courtiers and foolish pages said, "We do."

Criticus then said:

"Then we (reserving unto Delia's [Cynthia's] grace her farther pleasure, and to Arete what Delia grants) thus do sentence you.

"Your sentence is that from this place, for penance known of all, since you have drunk so deeply of Self-Love, you, two and two, singing a palinode [a song of repentance], will march to your separate homes by Niobe's stone, and offer up two tears, one from each eye, apiece thereon, so that it may change the name, as you must change, and of a stone be called Weeping Cross because it stands cross of Cynthia's highway, one of whose names is sacred Trivia [three ways meeting]."

Each of the foolish courtiers and foolish pages has a "home" by the Fountain of Self-Love because they are so full of Self-Love.

Criticus continued:

"And after this penance is thus performed, you must pass in like set order, not as Midas did to wash his gold off into Tagus' stream, but you must pass to the Well of Knowledge, Helicon, and wash off your Self-Love."

Midas was granted his wish that everything he touched would turn to gold, but it turned out to be a curse because his food and drink and his son turned to gold. Washing in the Tagus River cured his curse. Afterward, gold was found in the river.

The Helicon was a mountain that was sacred to the Muses. On the Helicon were sacred fountains.

Criticus continued:

"At Helicon, once you are purged of your present maladies, which are neither few nor slender, you will become such as you eagerly would seem to be; and you will then return, offering your service to great Cynthia.

"This is your sentence, if the goddess please

"To ratify it with her high consent;

"The scope of wise mirth unto fruit is bent."

Cynthia said:

"We do approve thy judgment, Criticus.

"Mercury, thy true propitious friend, a deity who is beloved by us second to Jove, will undertake to see thy judgment exactly done.

"And for this service of discovery performed by thee, in honor of our name, we vow to reward it with such due grace as shall become our bounty and thy place.

"Princes who wish their people should do well

"Must at themselves begin, as at the heads of fountains;

"For men by their example pattern out

"Their imitations and regard of laws.

"A virtuous court, a world to virtue draws."

Cynthia, Arete, Timè, Phronesis, Thauma, and Criticus exited.

PALINODE

A palinode is a song in which a previous viewpoint is retracted.

The Reformed Self-Lovers renounce their Self-Love in this song:

Amorphus sang:

"From Spanish shrugs, French faces, smirks, irpes, and all affected humors."

[Spanish shrugs and French faces are affectations.]

["Irpes" may mean "sinful sexual temptations."]

The Chorus of Reformed Self-Lovers sang:

"Good Mercury defend us!"

Phantaste sang:

"From secret friends, sweet servants, loves, doves, and such fantastic humors."

The Chorus of Reformed Self-Lovers sang:

"Good Mercury defend us!"

Amorphus sang:

"From stabbing of arms, flap-dragons, healths [toasts], whiffs [smoking tobacco], and all such swaggering humors."

[A lover could stab his own arm and drink his own blood as a sign of devotion to the woman he loved.]

[Flap-dragons are raisins that have been soaked in burning brandy and then are eaten.]

The Chorus of Reformed Self-Lovers sang:

"Good Mercury defend us!"

Phantaste sang:

"From waving of fans, coy glances, glicks [sexy glances], cringes [bows], and all such simpering humors."

The Chorus of Reformed Self-Lovers sang:

"Good Mercury defend us!"

Amorphus sang:

"From making love by attorney [indirectly], courting of puppets, and paying for new acquaintance."

[Puppets are decoys; a lover may court a servant in order to gain access to the lady whom the servant serves.]

The Chorus of Reformed Self-Lovers sang:

"Good Mercury defend us!"

Phantaste sang:

"From perfumed dogs, monkeys, sparrows, dildos, and paraquitos [parakeets]."

[Dildos are sometimes shaped like animals.]

The Chorus of Reformed Self-Lovers sang:

"Good Mercury defend us!"

Amorphus sang:

"From wearing bracelets of hair [a kind of love-token], shoe-ties, gloves, garters, and rings with posies."

The Chorus of Reformed Self-Lovers sang:

"Good Mercury defend us!"

Phantaste sang:

"From pargeting [plastering on of makeup], painting [putting on makeup], slicking [making glossy], glazing [making sleek], and renewing old rivelled [wrinkled] faces."

The Chorus of Reformed Self-Lovers sang:

"Good Mercury defend us!"

Amorphus sang:

"From squiring [escorting] to tilt-yards [jousting yards], playhouses, pageants, and all such public places."

The Chorus of Reformed Self-Lovers sang:

"Good Mercury defend us!"

Phantaste sang:

"From entertaining one gallant to gull [fool] another, and making fools of either."

The Chorus of Reformed Self-Lovers sang:

"Good Mercury defend us!"

Amorphus sang:

"From belying [lying about] ladies' [sexual] favors, noblemen's countenance, coining counterfeit employments, vain-glorious taking to them other men's services, and all self-loving humors."

The Chorus of Reformed Self-Lovers sang:

"Good Mercury defend us!"

Cantus [Song] Sung By All the Reformed Self-Lovers

"Now each one of us [will] dry his or her weeping eyes,

"*And to the Well of Knowledge make haste;*
"*Where purged of our maladies,*
"*We may of sweeter waters taste,*
"*And with refined voice report,*
"*The grace of Cynthia and her court.*"

EPILOGUE

The Epilogue (person who spoke the epilogue) was Criticus, who had went in (gone backstage) before the Palinode was sung.

The Epilogue said:

"Gentles, be't [be it] known to you, since I went in

"I am turned rhymer, and do thus begin:

"The author, jealous [doubtful] how your sense doth [does] take

"His travails, hath [has] enjoined me to make

"Some short and ceremonious epilogue,

"But if I yet know what, I am a rogue.

"He ties me to such laws, as quite distract

"My thoughts, and would a year of time exact [require].

"I neither must be faint, remiss, nor sorry,

"Sour, serious, confident, nor peremptory,

"But betwixt [between] these. Let's see; to lay the blame

"Upon the children's action [child-actors' performance; the play was performed by children], that were lame [would be a lame idea].

"To crave your favors with a begging knee,

"Were [Would be] to distrust the writer's faculty [Ben Jonson's ability as a playwright].

"To promise better at the next we bring,

"Prorogues [Defers] disgrace, commends not anything.

"Stiffly to stand on this, and proudly approve

"The play, might tax [accuse] the maker of Self-Love."

The maker — playwright — of *The Fountain of Self-Love* is Ben Jonson.

The Epilogue continued:

"I'll only speak what I have heard him say:

"'By God, 'tis [it is] good, and if you like't [like it], you may."

***

Ecce rubet quidam, pallet, stupet, oscitat, odit.

   Hoc volo: nunc nobis carmina nostra placent.

*

The Latin quotes Martial's *Epigrammatica* 60:3-4.

The entire poem is four lines:

Laudat, amat, cantat nostros mea Roma libellos,

Meque sinus omnes, me manus omnis habet.

Ecce rubet quidam, pallet, stupet, oscitat, odit.

Hoc volo: nunc nobis carmina nostra placent.

Translation:

Rome praises, loves, sings my little books

Every bosom has me, every hand has me.

Look! A man blushes, pales, is astonished, yawns, and hates.

I want this: Now our songs please us.

NOTES

— Cast of Characters —

Whetstone. Whetstones were hung around the necks of liars as a punishment.

Here is some information about whetstones from "Whetstones for Dull Wits and Liars" by saucyindexer:

Punishment of the Pillory and Whetstone

In the Letter Books of the City of London from 1412 there is an account of the deceit of William Blakeney, a shuttlemaker. "Under the guise of sanctity" and also barefoot and with long hair he pretended to be a hermit and "under colour of such falsehood he had received many good things from divers persons." As a skilled craftsman he was capable of supporting himself but for six years he "lived by such lies, falsities, and deceits, so invented by him, to the defrauding of the people."

"It was adjudged that said William should be put upon the pillory for three market-days, there to remain for one hour each day, the reason for the same being there proclaimed; and he was to have, in the meantime, whetstone hung from his neck."

Source of Above: saucyindexer, "Whetstones for Dull Wits and Liars." Lost Art Press. 5 October 2019
< https://blog.lostartpress.com/2019/10/05/__trashed/ >.

— 2.3 —

He's the very mint

    of compliment; all his behaviours are printed, his face is another volume

    of essays, and his beard an Aristarchus.

(2.3.68-70)

Source of Above:

The Cambridge Edition of the Works of Ben Jonson

7 Volume Set. Volume 1.

Ben Jonson (Author), David Bevington (Editor), Martin Butler (Editor), Ian Donaldson (Editor).

Cambridge University Press, 2012. Print. P. 479.

The following information comes from "1500s: The Elizabethan Ruff, Manicured Beards and Arum Starch #2":

Beard Starching.

Beard starching. Never done it? The Elizabeth era was the prime time for men to display their creativity in beard shaping, a somewhat neglected manicure amongst the gentlemen of today. A man wishing to sculpt his beard into a suitably fashionable and attractive shape had to take into account a number of considerations. Firstly there were the Elizabethan class dictates, so that where he lived and what profession he held played an important role in how his beard might be manipulated. Such important social signals were not to be overlooked. That decided, he was then free to enter the constantly changing fashion race of sculpting his beard into different angles, shapes, cuts, coils and contortions.

'having starched their beards most curiously...'

To ensure such facial architecture would remain in place, men would stiffen their beards with starch. Now, there is a persistent rumour that it was specifically Arum starch that was used for this. The source of this is

163

usually Cecil Prime, who refers to a preface by Thomas Nashe in Robert Greene's Menaphon *of 1589. The actual sentence is this:*

'Sufficeth them to bodge up a blank verse with ifs and ands, and otherwhile, for recreation after their candle-stuff, having starched their beards most curiously, to make a peripatetical path into the inner parts of the City, and spend two or three hours in turning over French dowdy, where they attract more infection in one minute than they can do eloquence all days of their life by conversing with any authors of like argument'.

Source of Above Information:
"1500s: The Elizabethan Ruff, Manicured Beards and Arum Starch #2". © 2010 Lynden Swift.
https://wildarum.co.uk/Blog/files/
c8c844e2670b8500fc0eaa0c3d303385-30.html
Some information about starched ruffs is here:
https://wildarum.co.uk/Blog/files/
1cc90517ca09b994e1839eec150566cb-29.html

— 3.4 —

Do deeds worthy the hurdle or the wheel,
(3.4.29)
Source of Above:
The Cambridge Edition of the Works of Ben Jonson
7 Volume Set. Volume 1.
Ben Jonson (Author), David Bevington (Editor), Martin Butler (Editor), Ian Donaldson (Editor).
Cambridge University Press, 2012. Print. P. 494.
The information below comes from the Wikipedia article "Breaking wheel":

*Those convicted as murderers and/or robbers to be executed by the wheel, sometimes termed to be "wheeled" or **broken on the wheel**, would be taken to a public stage scaffold site and tied to the floor. The execution wheel was typically a large wooden spoked wheel, the same as was used on wooden transport carts and carriages (often with iron rim), sometimes purposely modified with a rectangular iron thrust attached and extending blade-like from part of the rim. The primary goal of the first act was the agonizing mutilation of the body, not death. Therefore, the most common form would start with breaking the leg bones. To this end, the executioner dropped the execution wheel on the shinbones of the convicted person and then worked his way up to the arms. Here, rhythm and number of beatings were prescribed in each case, sometimes also the number of spokes on the wheel. To increase its effect, often sharp-edged timbers were placed under the convict's joints. Later, there were devices in which the convicted person could be "harnessed". Although not commonplace, the executioner could be instructed to execute the convicted person at the end of the first act, by aiming for the neck or heart in a "coup de grace". Even less often, this occurred immediately from the start (from the head down).*

In the second act, the body was braided into another wooden spoked wheel, which was possible through the broken limbs, or tied to the wheel. The wheel was then erected on a mast or pole, like a crucifixion. After this, the executioner was permitted to decapitate or garrotte the convicted if need be. Alternatively, fire was kindled under the wheel, or the "wheeled" convict was simply thrown into a fire. Occasionally, a small gallows was set up on the wheel, for example, if there were a guilty verdict for theft in addition to murder.

Since the body remained on the wheel after execution, left to scavenging animals, birds and decay, this form of punishment, like the ancient crucifixion, had a sacral function beyond death: according to the belief at that time, this would hinder transition from death to resurrection.

If the convict fell from the wheel still alive or the execution failed in some other way, such as the wheel itself breaking or falling from its placement, it was interpreted as God's intervention. There exist votive imaegs of saved victims of the wheel, and there is literature on how best to treat such sustained injuries.

The survival time after being "wheeled" or "broken" could be extensive. Accounts exist of a 14th-century murderer who remained conscious for three days after undergoing the punishment. In 1348, during the time of the Black Death, a Jewish man named Bona Dies underwent the punishment. The authorities stated he remained conscious for four days and nights afterwards. In 1581, the possibly fictitious German serial killer Christman Genipperteinga remained conscious for nine days on the breaking wheel before expiring, having been deliberately kept alive with "strong drink"

Alternatively, the condemned were spreadeagled and broken on a saltire, a cross consisting of two wooden beams nailed in an "X" shape, after which the victim's mangled body might be displayed on the wheel.

Source of Above: "Breaking wheel." Wikipedia. Accessed 8 January 2022. < https://en.wikipedia.org/wiki/Breaking_wheel >

— 3.5 —

ASOTUS
Well, sir, I'll enter again; her title shall be 'My dear Lindabrides'.
AMORPHUS
Lindabrides?
(3.5.24-25)
The University of Michigan has put this book (*The Mirror of Knighthood*, translated by Robert Parry) online:

> *The second part of the first booke of the Myrrour of knighthood in which is prosecuted the illustrious deedes of the knight of the Sunne, and his brother Rosicleer, sonnes vnto the Emperour Trebatio of Greece: with the valiant deedes of armes of sundry worthie knights, very delightfull to bee read, and nothing hurtfull to bee regarded. Now newly translated out of Spanish into our vulgar tongue by R.P.*

> Ortuñez de Calahorra, Diego. aut, R. P., fl. 1583-1586., Parry, Robert, fl. 1540-1612, attributed name., Parke, Robert, fl. 1588, attributed name.

https://quod.lib.umich.edu/e/eebo/A08545.0001.001/1:5?rgn=div1;view=fulltext
You can find the online Table of Contents here:
https://quod.lib.umich.edu/e/eebo/A08545.0001.001/1:5?rgn=div1;view=toc
Here is some information about Lindabrides from *Dictionary of Phrase and Fable*:

> *A heroine in The Mirror of Knighthood, whose name at one time was a synonym for a kept mistress, in which sense it was used by [Sir Walter] Scott, [in his novels]* Kenilworth *and* Woodstock.

Source: *Dictionary of Phrase and Fable*, E. Cobham Brewer, 1894.

— **3.5** —

If reguardant [Demonstrating], *then maintain your station, brisk and irpe,* 65
    show the supple motion of your pliant body, but, in chief, of your knee and
    hand, which cannot but arride her proud humour exceedingly.
(3.5.65-67)
Source of Above:
The Cambridge Edition of the Works of Ben Jonson
7 Volume Set. Volume 1.
Ben Jonson (Author), David Bevington (Editor), Martin Butler (Editor), Ian Donaldson (Editor).
Cambridge University Press, 2012. Print. P. 498.

In my opinion, "irpe" is a typo for "ripe," which means, according to *The Oxford Dictionary*:

> *Of grain, fruit, etc.: having developed to the point of readiness for harvesting and eating, or for the dispersal of seed for propagation; that is at the full extent of natural growth.*

> *Of a person: fully developed in body or mind; mature, fully grown; (also) †marriageable (obsolete).*

The lady is "reguardant," which means, according to the *Oxford English Dictionary*:

> *Heraldry. Of an animal: looking backwards over the shoulder. Also: (in early use) = guardant adj. 2[1]. Chiefly used postpositively.*

> *Observant, watchful, attentive; contemplative.*

What may be happening here is that the lady is considering whether Asotus would be a possible sex partner. She could be looking at him attentively to determine that. If she is looking backwards over her shoulder at him, she could be showing off her figure, offering — presenting — it to him.

---

1. *https://www-oed-com.proxy.library.ohio.edu/view/Entry/82139#eid2283364*

Asotus, in turn, is showing off "the supple motion of [his] pliant body, but, in chief, of [his] knee and hand."

In the missionary position, his knees and hands would be on the bed.

Asotus' doing this would "arride her proud humour exceedingly."

"Arride" means "gratify," and there could be a pun on him gratifying her by riding her.

This is one meaning of "proud," according to the *Oxford English Dictionary*:

> *Feeling greatly honoured, pleased, or satisfied by something which or someone who does one credit; acutely aware of some honour done to oneself, taking pride in something.* Also more generally (chiefly in early use): gratified, pleased, glad (now regional).

In the Palinode, "irpes" may mean "sinful sexual temptations."

— Whole Play —

Self-Love is Pride.

Pride is the foundation of all sins; pride makes a person think that he or she is the center of the universe. These are the seven deadly sins, and these are illustrations of how these sinners think:

1) Pride — A sinner who is guilty of Pride thinks, "I am the center of the universe, and I am better than other people. Quite simply, I am more important than other people."

2) Envy — A sinner who is guilty of Envy thinks, "I am the center of the universe, and if you have something I want, I envy you."

3) Wrath — A sinner who is guilty of Wrath thinks, "Because I am the center of the universe, everything ought to go my way, and when it does not, I get angry."

4) Sloth — A sinner who is guilty of Sloth thinks, "I am the center of the universe, so I don't have to work at something. Other people can do my work for me, and/or they can give me credit for work I have not done because if I had done the work, I would have done it excellently."

5) Avariciousness and Prodigality — A sinner who is guilty of Avariciousness or Prodigality thinks, "I am the center of the universe, so I deserve to have what I want. If I want money, I get money and never spend it, or if I want the things that money can buy, then I spend every penny I can make or borrow to get what I want. Either way, I deserve to have what I want."

6) Gluttony — A sinner who is guilty of Gluttony thinks, "I am the center of the universe, so I deserve these three extra pieces of pie every night. This is my reward for myself for being so fabulous."

7) Lust — A sinner who is guilty of Lust thinks, "I am the center of the universe, so my needs take precedence over the needs of everyone else. If I want to get laid, it's OK if I lie to get someone in bed and never call that person afterward. My sexual pleasure is more important than the hurt of someone who realizes that he or she has been used."

In Dante's *Purgatory*, the repentant sinners purge these sins in the order of the sins' evil, starting with Pride.

By the way, according to Dante's *Inferno*:

What is at the center of the universe?

The Earth.

What is at the center of the Earth?

Lucifer.

What is at the center of Lucifer?

His rectum.

What is at the center of Lucifer's rectum?

Former food that isn't food anymore.

***

Perhaps, when Philautia, whose name means "Self-Love," drinks from the Fountain of Self-Love, the water has no effect on her. She already loves herself above all others.

Supposedly, when the others drink from the Fountain of Self-Love, they begin to love themselves above all others.

Actually, they all seem full of Self-Love even before drinking from the Fountain of Self-Love.

Amorphus is the first to drink from the Fountain of Self-Love, and he immediately says some egotistic things about himself, but even before he drinks the cursed water he is shocked that the nymph Echo runs away from him.

Still, after drinking from the Fountain of Self-Love, some of the drinkers say that they are better than Cynthia. Drinking from the Fountain of Self-Love seems to intensify their Self-Love.

Appendix A: Fair Use

This communication uses information that I have downloaded and adapted from the WWW. I will not make a dime from it. The use of this information is consistent with fair use:

§ 107. Limitations on exclusive rights: Fair use

Release date: 2004-04-30

Notwithstanding the provisions of sections 106 and 106A, the fair use of a copyrighted work, including such use by reproduction in copies or phonorecords or by any other means specified by that section, for purposes such as criticism, comment, news reporting, teaching (including multiple copies for classroom use), scholarship, or research, is not an infringement of copyright. In determining whether the use made of a work in any particular case is a fair use the factors to be considered shall include —

(1) the purpose and character of the use, including whether such use is of a commercial nature or is for nonprofit educational purposes;

(2) the nature of the copyrighted work;

(3) the amount and substantiality of the portion used in relation to the copyrighted work as a whole; and

(4) the effect of the use upon the potential market for or value of the copyrighted work.

The fact that a work is unpublished shall not itself bar a finding of fair use if such finding is made upon consideration of all the above factors.

Source of Fair Use information:

<http://www.law.cornell.edu/uscode/17/107.html>

Appendix B: About the Author

It was a dark and stormy night. Suddenly a cry rang out, and on a hot summer night in 1954, Josephine, wife of Carl Bruce, gave birth to a boy — me. Unfortunately, this young married couple allowed Reuben Saturday, Josephine's brother, to name their first-born. Reuben, aka "The Joker," decided that Bruce was a nice name, so he decided to name me Bruce Bruce. I have gone by my middle name — David — ever since.

Being named Bruce David Bruce hasn't been all bad. Bank tellers remember me very quickly, so I don't often have to show an ID. It can be fun in charades, also. When I was a counselor as a teenager at Camp Echoing Hills in Warsaw, Ohio, a fellow counselor gave the signs for "sounds like" and "two words," then she pointed to a bruise on her leg twice. Bruise Bruise? Oh yeah, Bruce Bruce is the answer!

Uncle Reuben, by the way, gave me a haircut when I was in kindergarten. He cut my hair short and shaved a small bald spot on the back of my head. My mother wouldn't let me go to school until the bald spot grew out again.

Of all my brothers and sisters (six in all), I am the only transplant to Athens, Ohio. I was born in Newark, Ohio, and have lived all around Southeastern Ohio. However, I moved to Athens to go to Ohio University and have never left.

At Ohio U, I never could make up my mind whether to major in English or Philosophy, so I got a bachelor's degree with a double major in both areas, then I added a Master of Arts degree in English and a Master of Arts degree in Philosophy. Yes, I have my MAMA degree.

Currently, and for a long time to come (I eat fruits and veggies), I am spending my retirement writing books such as *Nadia Comaneci: Perfect 10*, *The Funniest People in Dance*, *Homer's* Iliad: *A Retelling in Prose*, and *William Shakespeare's* Othello: *A Retelling in Prose*.

By the way, my sister Brenda Kennedy writes romances such as *A New Beginning* and *Shattered Dreams*.

Appendix C: Some Books by David Bruce

Retellings of a Classic Work of Literature

Arden of Faversham: *A Retelling*

Ben Jonson's The Alchemist: *A Retelling*

Ben Jonson's The Arraignment, or Poetaster: *A Retelling*

Ben Jonson's Bartholomew Fair: *A Retelling*

Ben Jonson's The Case is Altered: *A Retelling*

Ben Jonson's Catiline's Conspiracy: *A Retelling*

Ben Jonson's The Devil is an Ass: *A Retelling*

Ben Jonson's Epicene: *A Retelling*

Ben Jonson's Every Man in His Humor: *A Retelling*

Ben Jonson's Every Man Out of His Humor: *A Retelling*

Ben Jonson's The Fountain of Self-Love, or Cynthia's Revels: *A Retelling*

Ben Jonson's The Magnetic Lady, or Humors Reconciled: *A Retelling*

Ben Jonson's The New Inn, or The Light Heart: *A Retelling*

Ben Jonson's Sejanus' Fall: *A Retelling*

Ben Jonson's The Staple of News: *A Retelling*

Ben Jonson's A Tale of a Tub: *A Retelling*

Ben Jonson's Volpone, or the Fox: *A Retelling*

Christopher Marlowe's Complete Plays: Retellings

Christopher Marlowe's Dido, Queen of Carthage: *A Retelling*

Christopher Marlowe's Doctor Faustus: *Retellings of the 1604 A-Text and of the 1616 B-Text*

Christopher Marlowe's Edward II: *A Retelling*

Christopher Marlowe's The Massacre at Paris: *A Retelling*

Christopher Marlowe's The Rich Jew of Malta: *A Retelling*

Christopher Marlowe's Tamburlaine, Parts 1 and 2: *Retellings*

Dante's Divine Comedy: *A Retelling in Prose*

Dante's Inferno: *A Retelling in Prose*

Dante's Purgatory: *A Retelling in Prose*

Dante's Paradise: *A Retelling in Prose*

The Famous Victories of Henry V: *A Retelling*

From the Iliad *to the* Odyssey: *A Retelling in Prose of Quintus of Smyrna's* Posthomerica

George Chapman, Ben Jonson, and John Marston's Eastward Ho! *A Retelling*

George Peele's The Arraignment of Paris: *A Retelling*

George Peele's The Battle of Alcazar: *A Retelling*

George Peele's David and Bathsheba, and the Tragedy of Absalom: *A Retelling*

George Peele's Edward I: *A Retelling*

George Peele's The Old Wives' Tale: *A Retelling*

George-a-Greene: *A Retelling*

William Shakespeare's 1 Henry IV, aka Henry IV, Part 1: *A Retelling in Prose*

William Shakespeare's 2 Henry IV, aka Henry IV, Part 2: *A Retelling in Prose*

William Shakespeare's 1 Henry VI, aka Henry VI, Part 1: *A Retelling in Prose*

William Shakespeare's 2 Henry VI, aka Henry VI, Part 2: *A Retelling in Prose*

William Shakespeare's 3 Henry VI, aka Henry VI, Part 3: *A Retelling in Prose*

William Shakespeare's All's Well that Ends Well: *A Retelling in Prose*

William Shakespeare's Antony and Cleopatra: *A Retelling in Prose*

William Shakespeare's As You Like It: *A Retelling in Prose*

William Shakespeare's The Comedy of Errors: *A Retelling in Prose*

William Shakespeare's Coriolanus: *A Retelling in Prose*

William Shakespeare's Cymbeline: *A Retelling in Prose*

William Shakespeare's Hamlet: *A Retelling in Prose*

William Shakespeare's Henry V: *A Retelling in Prose*

William Shakespeare's Henry VIII: *A Retelling in Prose*

William Shakespeare's Julius Caesar: *A Retelling in Prose*

William Shakespeare's King John: *A Retelling in Prose*

William Shakespeare's King Lear: *A Retelling in Prose*

William Shakespeare's Love's Labor's Lost: *A Retelling in Prose*

William Shakespeare's Macbeth: *A Retelling in Prose*

William Shakespeare's Measure for Measure: *A Retelling in Prose*

William Shakespeare's The Merchant of Venice: *A Retelling in Prose*

William Shakespeare's The Merry Wives of Windsor: *A Retelling in Prose*

William Shakespeare's A Midsummer Night's Dream: *A Retelling in Prose*

William Shakespeare's Much Ado About Nothing: *A Retelling in Prose*

William Shakespeare's Othello: *A Retelling in Prose*

William Shakespeare's Pericles, Prince of Tyre: *A Retelling in Prose*

William Shakespeare's Richard II: *A Retelling in Prose*

William Shakespeare's Richard III: *A Retelling in Prose*

William Shakespeare's Romeo and Juliet: *A Retelling in Prose*

William Shakespeare's The Taming of the Shrew: *A Retelling in Prose*

William Shakespeare's The Tempest: *A Retelling in Prose*

William Shakespeare's Timon of Athens: *A Retelling in Prose*

William Shakespeare's Titus Andronicus: *A Retelling in Prose*

William Shakespeare's Troilus and Cressida: *A Retelling in Prose*

William Shakespeare's Twelfth Night: *A Retelling in Prose*

William Shakespeare's The Two Gentlemen of Verona: *A Retelling in Prose*

William Shakespeare's The Two Noble Kinsmen: *A Retelling in Prose*

William Shakespeare's The Winter's Tale: *A Retelling in Prose*